THE PARAFFIN GLOVE AND THE DARK GENIUS

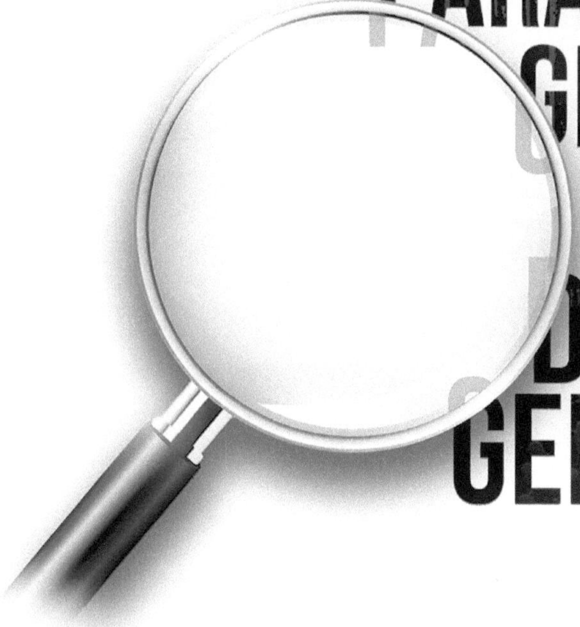

DAVID BARSKY

978-1-960197-54-2 (Paperback)
978-1-960197-55-9 (eBook)

DEDICATION

I dedicate this book to my parents who I loved and miss, and for their moral support.

I want to thank my friend Mike Tenuto for his moral support and Andy Kahn my music mentor, and other friends.

I also dedicate this book to my dear friend Deirdre Villa

TABLE OF CONTENTS

THE
PARAFFIN
GLOVE

CHAPTER ONE

It was four years ago in March of 2006 when a young woman became a victim of a crime. Her name, no one quite knows. The young lady lights up any room she walks into. But no one knows her secret.

The phone rings and Detective Tamara Jones of the Egg Harbor Police Department answers the phone. Calling the police is Beth Stein. "Officer I just discovered the remains of a young male," Officer Jones, "Excuse me, you say that you just found the remains of a young male, but how do you know the person is dead, are you a doctor or nurse or some other expert?"

"I'm calling to report that there is a young male I believe he's dead and you won't let me talk." The detective doesn't just interrupt Ms. Stein;

Detective Jones doesn't give Ms. Stein the opportunity to state where Ms. Stein found the remains. Ms. Stein calls again to speak to a detective in the violent crime unit and Detective Fisher asks, "How can I help you Ms. Stein?"

"I tried to report that I found the remains of a young male and was cut off by Officer Jones. The remains are in a field above Main Street Detective Fisher. You have to walk up a path and you will see the remains over on your right hand side."

"Thank you Ms. Stein and I apologize for the way you were treated. I will be there in fifteen minutes with another detective. Will you be able to meet us on the street where the path is?"

"Yes I will."

"Amy, I just received a call that a young male has been found dead on Main Street by a woman named Beth Stein and I want you to come with me."

"I'm ready Mike let's go. You're driving right?"

"Yes Amy, I'm driving. I have the keys since I already signed out a car."

"Okay Mike. You drive faster then I do."

"You're really funny Amy."

Detective Goldstein was promoted after solving a sex crime that took place at the Sunset Motel near Brick Township in South Jersey and scoring one of the highest grades in New Jersey's history of law enforcement. "Amy, we are here. The yellow tape has already been setup to keep curious residents and visitors from disturbing the crime scene so let's checkout the crime scene." The male body is that of a 24 year old with dark brown hair, thin to medium build, wearing jeans and a tee shirt that says "Live Free or Die." The Crime Scene Unit leader Helen Ross, "Look detectives the victim is wearing a religious symbol on his gold chain. It's a Jewish star."

"What does that tell you Helen?" Ross, "That our murder victim was not killed by a thief. Helen Ross goes through their pockets and finds a wallet belonging to the victim. You see detectives I was right, a thief didn't kill this young man."

"Why did she wink at you like that?"

"We tease each other from time to time."

"How do you think he died, after all, there's no bullet or knife wounds."

"I can't tell you that right now, but I can tell both of you this young man has been here since 7:00 AM this morning. "Are you certified as a medical examiner?"

"I'm the coroner and earned my degree in medicine three years ago. I use to put in twelve to fourteen hour shifts but now I spend more time with my daughter Pamela."

"How old is your daughter?"

"She's 10 years old."

"How long will it take for you to determine how this young male died?"

"It could take me up to a day."

"Are you going to do the autopsy yourself?"

"Yes Detective, I'm going to do the autopsy myself."

"Please don't take me the wrong way, but if he were your son, would you want to wait a day, two days, or more to find out how your child died and when the case would proceed?"

"That's interesting, and I think insulting, that you would imply that I'm in no hurry to discover how this young life was brought to an abrupt end. You can't rush science Detective. May I suggest that you stick with what you know." Fisher, "Helen, can I talk with you a moment? Please don't take Amy the wrong way. She really does mean well and wants to catch the person responsible."

"Then she should give me the time to do my job correctly."

"Amy, let's head back to the office. I'll fill you in." Detective Goldstein, "I bet she's pissed at me, isn't she?"

"She wants you to leave her alone to do her job correctly. Helen takes a lot of pride in what she does Amy. I've known Helen for about five years. She's not angry with you, or you would have gotten an ear full." Detective Goldstein, "How long do you think it will take for us to get any information from Dr. Ross?"

"Actually Amy, Helen will probably call us later today or tomorrow morning. You don't rush an autopsy."

After returning to the police department the two detectives are approached by their Captain, Lou Costello. "What happened with Tamara Jones?"

"A woman named Beth Stein called here to inform us that she found the remains of a young male. When she called the second time I answered the phone. Ms. Stein told me that when she called originally she was not able to even explain where she found the remains of the person. Detective Jones was rude and kept cutting Ms. Stein off from describing what she found. So after getting the location of the remains of the victim I told Amy to take a ride with me to the crime scene since Tamara was rude to a possible witness and Amy has better interpersonal skills with perspective witnesses then Tamara, and captain, you weren't here yet."

The phone rings and Helen Ross is on the other end. "Come down to the lab Mike."

"You got something?"

"See you when you get down here."

Fisher, Goldstein, and Costello head to the lab leaving Detective Jones to complete reports as a punishment for acting unprofessional with a perspective witness."

"I wanted to take this time to apologize for being rude and didn't mean any disrespect to you."

"Thank you Amy. Your apology is appreciated and accepted. Now, let me share some information with you that is really strange:

Sharon who is my new assistant and I found a mark left by a syringe at the brain stem."

"That had to hurt real bad."

"Actually Mike, it was after the shot that he suffered. At least five minutes later there were three possible effects from the injection. The first could have been a burning sensation, the second, a real cold feeling like a brain freeze; and third, could have been a feeling that the victim's head was going to explode"

"Were there any signs that he had intercourse with someone?"

"I believe the victim did have intercourse within the past 24 hours. Here's something else for you to include in your investigation, there are no finger or hand prints."

"That's pretty strange."

"Even in cases like this one where you find a victim with his clothes on, there is usually a hand print or foot print, even if there are no fingerprints."

"Helen, what could someone do in order not to leave a print behind other then latex gloves, which we know from experience can still leave a hand print or residue?"

"To be honest with you Mike, I don't know of anything right now that someone could use and not leave any type of hand or fingerprint."

"When you come up with something can you let us know as soon as possible?"

"Absolutely Mike. You got something on your mind?"

"Yes Helen, I do."

"Do you want to share with us Mike what's on your mind?"

"Helen, can you bring up on the computer different substances similar to latex that can be used for gloves?"

"Let's see Mike. entering polymers and no information."

"How about fabrics Helen?"

"Entering flexible gloves made from cloth and no such data other then winter wear."

"Thanks Helen, I'll have to do a little more research myself."

Fisher and Goldstein's captain gives his detectives the time they need to use the Internet. Fisher "Amy let's use your expertise with the Internet to learn what types gloves are on the market that our un-sub could be using."

"Okay Mike. Let me enter surgical equipment and gloves. Nothing is coming up Mike."

"I could have almost bet that we would have gotten a hit."

"The product is something out of the ordinary."

At 4:30 PM Detective Tamara Jones leaves the office after Captain Costello told Officer Jones that she was written up for her poor conduct. "Hey Captain, I see Tamara just left and she was pretty angry."

"You know Mike this is the third time Tamara has been written up."

"I hope that my saying something earlier isn't playing a part in that?"

"No Mike, this is all on Tamara. She's almost out of here. The woman you spoke to that found the remains of that young male this morning, Ms. Stein, reported Tamara to the Chief's office."

"So Captain, Tamara's police career is almost over. You and I both know that Chief Braun is going to push for suspension without pay due to her poor conduct"

"Are her actions, a career ender?"

"For Tamara, she will be reassigned. This is the third time that Tamara is in trouble for her behavior and hindering a criminal investigation. We can't have this kind of conduct on the force."

"What a lousy attitude."

"It's not for you to worry about Amy. Besides, Mike will tell you that you're a professional that Tamara never was."

"Amy you need to reach into your soul more when talking with people like Helen. When it comes to interviewing witnesses you show some real depth to your heart when a family has lost a loved one. I think you are going to be a great detective, captain, or chief someday."

"Just remember us when you make it. I put in some good words with Chief Braun recently."

"You guys are awesome! I owe you."

"Guess what Amy?"

"What Mike?"

"We'll remind you."

"I'm sure you will Mike."

"Its getting late folks, tomorrow's another day." Detectives Fisher and Goldstein sign out for the evening and decide to have dinner at the Diamond Diner where Detective Fisher wants to share something with Detective Goldstein. "I really like you Amy. You're intelligent and you have confidence in yourself, you're extremely attractive and cute. I know it's not always a good idea to get involved with people you work with, but I wanted to ask if you would consider a relationship with me?"

"Are you kidding Mike? I'm really attracted to you but I have no experience with anyone in a committed relationship. Can we move slowly?"

"Absolutely Amy I'm looking for a long-term relationship and I enjoy following the holidays. I don't setup a Christmas tree for religious reasons, but for how pretty they look indoors and outdoors."

"You decorate a tree for the Christmas holidays, my father and brother will turn pale white when, or if I show them." Fisher," How will your mother feel?"

"I think my mom will really like you."

"I'll look forward to meeting her someday."

"I'll formerly introduce you when I feel more comfortable. But you have to take it easy with me Mike. If you do that, well, there's no telling how close the two of us will become."

"Amy, I'm not going to rush you, okay?"

"Thanks Mike." Detective Goldstein reaches towards Detective Fisher with her hands, while looking into his brown eyes. Mike Fisher has been a police official for five years and now 27 years old. He was one of very few people of Jewish ancestry who served in the Marines from the time he was 17 years old until he turned twenty two and recruited by the Egg Harbor Police Department right out of "The Corp."Detective Fisher wasn't an officer for very long when he was on patrol one night when he saw a man and woman in a newer Chevy Impala and appeared to him that a man was on top of a woman and had pulled her legs apart and she was trying to move her arms. He hadn't heard her scream but he still called for backup and requested a female police officer. A dispatcher named Sam Tuneski sent a rookie cop who had completed an independent study and classes on the subject of sex crimes. That officer was Amy Goldstein, who let the guy have it for trying to rip the girl's clothes off. It was then officer Goldstein who tried to get the girl in the Impala to file a complaint for sexual assault but the girl who called herself Barbara, didn't want to file charges, she just wanted the guy to back off. It turned out that the girl liked the guy but didn't want to be rushed.

When Detective Fisher thinks back to the day he first met then, rookie officer Goldstein, he now wonders if the girl in the car was actually afraid of what the guy would do if she screamed rape at the time, and after the past few years, she is now getting even. "Let's pay the check and get out of here."

"It's been a busy day Mike and I could use some sleep." The following morning the phone rings and wakes up Detective Goldstein. "Who is this?"

"Amy, this is Mike, and we got another body."

"Are you at the scene already?"

"No I'm not Amy, do you want me to pick you up?" Goldstein, "I'll be ready in five minutes Mike."

"I'll be there with two cups of coffee, light on cream and sugar?"

"That'll be great Mike."

Ten minutes later the door bell rings, and it's Detective Fisher. Hi Mike I'm ready to go."

"Let me fill you in Amy. According to the call I got at 6:00 AM, another young male has been found dead. This male was found dead in the backyard of a friend's home on Susquehanna Avenue in Ventnor. The Ventnor Police called because they know that we are working on a similar case according to an officer named Mark Testa."

"Why does that last name sound familiar?"

"Ready to go Amy."

"Let's get going Mike you're driving, since your more comfortable driving fast. "That's because I've had to Amy."

"Well, this time you have to get us there fast."

"Fasten your seat belt Amy."

Detective Fisher pushes the "pedal to the medal." He and Goldstein drive into Ventnor, where they catch up with Detective Testa whose been overseeing the crime scene. "Are you Fisher and Goldstein?"

"Are you Detective Testa?"

"Yes. We got a real good one for you. Young white male, 22 years old and found dead in their friend's backyard. His pants are unbuttoned but that's it. "You know what this reminds me of folks?"

"A movie?"

"That's exactly right. Sudden Impact, starring Clint Eastwood as Dirty Harry,"

"Come on guys let's keep our minds on the job. This male is quite similar to the last one."

"I think someone is out for revenge, and if it's true, who could it be?"

"I think you might be on the right track guys, but here's a good question for you, why isn't there any finger or hand prints?" Testa, "I found what might be the footprint of a suspect." There's a voice from the background. It's the voice of Rob Weston, an investment adviser. "That footprint might be mine. You might want to see if it matches my sneakers or Dockers. My wife Lynne and I live here and Joe had been a friend of ours for years. We've known Joe since we were kids, and we are heart broken. Lynne is really upset. She's gotten over the worse of it for now; but it's going to be really bad when his family has the viewing."

"What is Joe's last name?"

"His last name is Tapper."

"How old was your friend?" Weston, "Joe was 22 years old. Detective Testa got it right"

"I know my questions are quite personal but, we only want to find the person who is responsible for his death. Was your friend in a relationship with anyone?"

"He wasn't in a committed relationship with anyone."

"I have to ask this question, did your friend make anyone angry lately, like a former girlfriend or male friend?"

"Yes, but we don't know why"

"Were you thinking about conducting an investigation aside from ours?"

"No Detective, I had no intention of conducting my own investigation but was considering asking a private investigator to look into any enemies my friend may have had. "Do you feel that your friend may have made an enemy?"

"Joe confided in me that he had someone who was ticked off at him."

"Did your friend ever say who that might be and why?"

"No, I don't recall my friend saying who was or wasn't angry with him."

"Have you seen a big difference in his personality recently?" Weston, "He's been quiet lately. I want to see if Lynne feels like talking. Lynne, are you up to talking to the police regarding Joe's death?"

Lynne, "Officers, Joe was acting nervous lately. When he came over one day, and you were at the office Rob, Joe would look out the window from the living room. I asked Joe if he was okay, because he kept looking outside like someone was watching him, and then he seemed to chill out after having a cigarette on the front steps."

"I noticed your friend had a lot of calls on his cell phone. Could you identify any of these phone numbers for us?"

"It might take sometime to identify the phone numbers with the people who called him. Do you have the time right now?"

"I've got time while you go down the list of phone numbers, how about you two. "I'm willing to hang out for a while and learn who the phone numbers belong to, how about you Amy?"

"Mr. Weston, can you identify these phone numbers for us?"

"This phone number belongs to Brian Shafer this other phone number belongs to Gary Rosen, and Lynne, "Doesn't this phone number belong to Beth Zimmerman?"

"Rob, that's Beth's phone number and this is Sharon's phone number. I don't recognize this phone number."

"Thank you folks we'll checkout this phone number. Do the people listed on this phone live within a few miles from here?"

"All but the one we didn't recognize that are friends. These people are going to be distraught over his death." Testa "Thank you."

The detectives leave the Weston home; and Testa tells Goldstein, "My uncle was accused of many crimes over his lifetime, but he never did time for killing anyone as far as I know. I'm careful not to accuse people since my uncle was accused of doing terrible things." Goldstein, "Who was your uncle?"

"Amy, you have to ask who Detective Testa's uncle was? Testa, "My Uncle was Pete Testa."

"What happened to your uncle?"

"He was killed from a bomb connected to the screen door to his house."

"You're not kidding are you?"

"No Detective Goldstein, I'm not kidding. My uncle was considered part of the mafia. Like there's really a mafia. I'm originally from South Philadelphia and must admit, that I do miss not being able to walk down the street, or a couple of blocks to a diner, and taking a walk the opposite direction to the neighborhood bar and grill where I could get a good meal, a couple drinks, and be able to walk home. When I wanted to go to a hockey or ball game, the stadium was ten minutes away. If you ever go to South Philly and don't mind paying a good amount of money for an Italian dinner, check out the Saloon."

"That's an Italian restaurant?"

"It's an excellent place to go for Italian food in Philadelphia."

"Well folks; I need to get back to the office."

"Thanks for your help." Testa "Be safe out there."

The ME has taken the remains of Joe Tapper from the Weston home at 10 Susquehanna Avenue near the CVS Pharmacy in Ventnor, to the local morgue for autopsy. The two detectives learned from the local crime scene tech, that the deceased Joe Tapper has been dead for three hours, which means he died at 6:00 AM. Joe Tapper is the second young male found dead in two days. He too, had a needle mark found in the brain stem. Usually a crime scene unit does not inspect the remains of someone other then hairs, or bugs, or particles found on clothes around the body. "What do you think Mike about this homicide?"

"It's the same un-sub Amy." Detective's Fisher and Goldstein have left the crime scene and on their way back to the Egg Harbor Twp. Police Department when Detective Goldstein ask her partner "What's the killer filling the syringe with? "I don't know Amy but I bet Helen will find out." It's Sunday, and detectives Fisher and Goldstein are at the department trying to come up with a solid clue. "So far Amy, there are no fingerprints, no handprints, DNA of the suspect we are looking for. Is our suspect a female and a victim of rape?"

"I don't know Mike I've never worked on a case before where there were no clues. It's like we're chasing a ghost." Their captain walks in "Why are the two of you in the office today?"

"We are trying to come up with some clues or a profile of our un-sub. Why did you come in Captain?"

"When I left yesterday I forgot my cigars. I'm still waiting for a new bundle I ordered the other day and they should be coming soon. I'll see you guys on Tuesday unless you get another victim. Hopefully I won't here from either of you until then."

"You're going to let us handle this case on our own?"

"Why not Amy, you're more then capable, and you're working with Mike."

"If I can ask captain, what's happening with Tamara?"

"She's no longer with our unit."

"So, she's still with the department?"

"Yes Mike, Tamara is still with the department, but not with our unit. You and Goldstein need to concentrate on this case. Chief Braun might be paying us a visit on Tuesday or Wednesday. Hopefully by then we have some leads to go on."

"Captain, I think we are looking for a female between the ages of twenty one and twenty four years old." Detective Goldstein, "I think our killer is familiar with their surroundings, angry and knows their victims."

"So they knew our un-sub." Fisher, "I think our killer was a victim of rape, or bullying." Goldstein "Why no footprints?"

How is this person able to stick a syringe into the brain stem of their victims and they don't realize what they are about to do?"

"Well, we haven't found any bodily fluids as of yet. How is our suspect able to take the lives of their victims and leave without being noticed and if our unsub had sex with this victim, then why hasn't there been any DNA left behind, did they actually take the time to clean up the victim before they left?"

"I believe your right Mike. Our suspect is a female. Only a woman would clean up after herself."

"Yes Amy, our suspect is probably attractive, and probably educated."

"I believe that we should be looking for a young lady who dresses nicely. She doesn't wear clothes like Britney Spears. Her parents wouldn't allow it."

"She drives a fairly new car. It's probably a Honda, Toyota, or maybe even a Subaru. Her car is an automatic, is red, blue, or silver."

"Let's get out of here Mike. We should go back to Ventnor tomorrow and see if we can interview some of the neighbors where the Weston's live."

"We could get together for breakfast and ring some door bells."

"See you on Tuesday."

Its Sunday 1:00 PM, after getting into Detective Fisher's Ford Escape, Fisher ask: Detective Goldstein, "Would you be interested in cooking out at my place? We could buy a couple of steaks or some burgers at the market near my home?"

"That's fine Mike." Detective Fisher while off duty doesn't usually drive fast. He owns a Ford Escape that is green with a tan interior. "I've never had a case like this one before Amy. Most un-subs leave at least one or two clues at a crime scene. What kind of car do you drive Amy?"

"I own a car and plus a sport utility vehicle. My car is a Chevrolet Impala and it includes the on-star system." Like Detective Fisher, Goldstein also has a flashing light she is able to mount on her dashboard, or roof if necessary. "Let's go in the market and get a couple of steaks Amy." When they arrive at Fisher's home, there is a silver Honda Accord outside the Miller's home that is located across the street from Detective Fisher's place. "Amy, leave the steaks in the truck and come with me."

"What are we going to do?"

"We are going to check on my neighbors."

"Do you think something is wrong?"

"We watch out for each other around here Amy."

"What do you want me to do?"

"Stay by my side. Were going to ring the front door bell but stand to the side of the window that is in the front door. The two detectives reach the front door and Fisher rings the bell. There's no answer yet, and Fisher has never seen the silver Honda before. "Something's wrong Amy, I can feel it."

"Why don't we go around the back of the house Mike?"

"That's a good idea. The remains of the last victim were discovered in the backyard of his friend's place." The two detectives walk with caution to the rear of the house. Fisher and Goldstein reach the backyard where they find Gary Miller, the son of Brian and Beth Miller. "Mike, this kid is still breathing."

"Are you sure Amy?"

"I took a course through the Red Cross and this kid is breathing."

"Operator, I'm Detective Fisher of the Egg Harbor Twp. Police, and we need an ambulance at 232 Bay Road, there is a young male in distress." Shortly after Fisher ended the call, he and Goldstein could here an ambulance. Fisher walks to the front of the house to wave at the ambulance when he sees them coming down the road. Two males and female paramedics exit the vehicle and rush over to Gary Miller to begin treating him. Two male paramedics, Jim Huntz a Black male who works out three times a week and has earned nothing less then A's and B's in all his courses related to paramedics. Huntz, "We need to get this kid ready for transporting to the hospital. He's in shock." The second paramedic that arrived at the scene Ken Dobbs is quite happy being a paramedic. Dobbs, "Tina, this guy's breathing seems quite shallow to me." Tina Connors the head of the team and RN, "I'm going to place a breathing tube in this kid or I'm afraid we are going to lose him."

"Do you think this kid might die on us?"

"He's struggling to breathe. "Were going to lose him, his blood pressure and pulse are getting weaker. Nurse Connors, "I'm going to increase the amount of oxygen slowly and let's get this kid ready for transport to Atlantic Care: Memorial" Hospital Mainland. Goldstein, "Can you see if there is a needle mark on the brain stem?"

"Actually I cannot check that right now, but will make a note of this on the report."

"It's urgent that we know if there is a needle mark on the brain stem."

"I can't do anything here detective. I'm sure the hospital can assist with finding the needle hole you're so intent on finding."

"Nurse Connors, it's really important that we know as soon as possible if there is a needle mark on the brain stem. Two young males have been found dead with needle marks on the brain stem. Do you want to tell the parents of these victims or future victims that you had no interests in helping us with our investigation?" What if one of these young males was one of your relatives or if one of these guys was your boyfriend?"

"You made your point folks. I can lift his head up just a bit, but you're going to have to look quickly."

"Thank You Tina, can you assist Mike?"

"I'll move his hair a little. Do you have a flashlight, this will help you see?"

"I'm ready." Nurse Connors holds the young male's head up at a safe level while Detective Goldstein uses a small flashlight to see if there is a needle mark and Detective Fisher moves the hair with his fingers. "Wait a minute Mike."

"Do you see a needle mark?"

"I want a doctor to confirm this."

"I'm stating that you found what could be a needle mark on the brain stem."

"Isn't there a way to determine if what chemical was injected at the site of a needle mark?" Nurse Connors, "I don't know about that, but the chemical should show up in tests." After the Miller's son is placed in the ambulance and on his way to the hospital, Fisher's cell phone and its Helen Ross the ME. "Mike I found a large dose of chemical that raised the blood pressure of these individuals that killed them, and yes, they suffered but I can't tell you what the chemical was. I'll have to send a sample to the State Forensic lab."

"Amy and I just found another victim Helen but this kid is still alive right now. Gary Miller is the son of Brian and Harriet Miller. His parents are both doctors. "I sure hope the security is good at the hospital. You should ask the State Police if they could provide a trooper for security."

"Good idea Helen. Amy and I are going to the hospital."

"What did she learn Mike?"

"So far Helen said the chemical she found in the first two victims raised the blood pressure to the extent that they suffered prior to their death."

"So, how could this victim survive when the others didn't?"

"We are going to have to learn why."

"I'm just asking that question myself Mike. Haven't you ever done that?"

"Actually Amy I haven't. When I ask myself a question when other officers can hear me, I'm hoping for some input. Usually Lou, Groucho, Harry, or Carla will realize what I'm doing. You're new to our team and will soon have the opportunity to meet the others."

"You have a guy who works in our unit named Groucho?"

"He looks a little and can talk like Groucho Marx. The comedian from the 1930s to the 1970s" Fisher and Goldstein finally arrive at the hospital and Detective Fisher, "Can you stay in the hospital room with Gary Miller? I heard that you are one of the best when it comes to overseeing security. State Trooper Mike Jarwinsky "Thank you for the compliment Detective, I heard that you have an excellent reputation as well."

"Not like you Trooper Jarwinsky. I know my neighbor's son is going to be safe now." Trooper Jarwinsky, What's this kid's full name?"

"His name is Gary Miller and he's great at repairing cars." Detectives Fisher and Goldstein head back to Fisher's home to cook their steaks and prepare a salad. "Amy, would you like a Blue Hawaiian cooler?"

"Are they strong?"

"It depends on the person. If you haven't had one before, it might hit you faster. No pressure Amy, if you prefer a glass of ice tea that's fine. I might have some red wine? "You're looking in the refrigerator for red wine? I thought red wine is supposed to be served at room temperature?"

"I didn't realize you were so knowledgeable of wines Amy."

"The red wine I have is already open and that's why it's in the refrigerator. So what do you think of this case were working on Amy?"

"I agree with you Mike, were looking for a female and she is educated or at least very intelligent as we said before. I think she was hurt by the young males in some way."

"You mean like a gang rape?"

"I know what a gang rape is."

"Possibly: As I said before, it's a female who is getting revenge; and based on what happened to her I'm likely to be in support of her actions."

"Are you telling me that if she was raped you are likely to look the other way?"

"Did I say that I would look the other way? Amy, what I'm saying is that I'm more likely going to support her actions and urge a light jail sentence or time in a hospital. This way, the woman would get the help she needs so she doesn't do hard time."

"I would agree to that. As far as I care, if she was raped or maybe date raped, this woman should get some help."

"You know what Amy, I never thought that our suspect could be the victim of date rape and check on court records."

"Either did I Mike. We both screwed up on this one."

"We can fix this mistake Amy just by spending sometime tomorrow and checking court and arrest records."

"We could use your computer Mike to check on some records."

"You're right Amy. After dinner we could work in the living room or sit out back and use a laptop?" How do you like your steak?" Goldstein "Medium well: I like your place so far." I've had this place since my Uncle Frank was seriously injured but got back on his feet after two years."

"What does he do?"

"He works for the Federal Government Amy and I can't say much more."

"Why, is his work top secret"

"I really don't know exactly."

Fisher and Goldstein have dinner together and get to know one another better. Fisher takes Goldstein on a tour of his home, a rancher. The kitchen is quite large. There's a woodstove in one corner of the kitchen next to a round kitchen table that seats 5 to 6 people. Detective Fisher, "I use this Sharp microwave convection oven that allows me to broil, bake, and roast while saving electric Amy. The kitchen is done in burgundy and white. The knobs used to pull the kitchen cabinets open are pearl white and handcrafted wood. In the back yard, a deck made from solid pine that includes a stainless steel gas grille. When Detective Goldstein turns to her left she sees an enclosed room with one-way glass. "What's in that room?"

"Let me show you Amy. Fisher takes her hand and walks her over to the closed off porch, opens the door, turns on the light and there is a hot tub. "Wow Mike, I have one of these."

"When you want to, just let me know."

"What's the rest of this house like?"

Fisher has Goldstein turn around and see the garden "Look I grow grapes and strawberries."

"Why do you grow your own grapes?" I sometimes make my own red wine but for the most part I just like eating red grapes and I like strawberries."

"I love the way your home is setup Mike. Your house doesn't look this big from the outside and I like the second bedroom, study, guest bathroom, the master bedroom, bath and shower. "Let me show you a car I bought at an auction and then restored it."

"What kind of car is it?"

"It's a traditionally red 1980 Alfa Rameo Spider."

"Mike, can we work in the living room rather then the backyard."

"That's perfectly fine Amy." In the living room she can't help seeing a display case that includes a small statute of a rabbi, a menorah, a blue glass with a Jewish star to fill with wine for Elijah, used during the Passover Seder. There is a desk with a 22" flat screen monitor and an HP tower on the floor to the right. When you look to the right on the wall is a 52" LCD Sharp flat screen television. "I don't care much for cable television Amy so I opted for Satellite Television and cable for Internet service with a wireless router."

The two detectives become close friends, and possibly a future couple. "Okay Mike let me use your computer to perform searches to see if we can find court cases involving rape, and date rapes."

"Has any judge allowed for an accused rapist or group accused of rape to walk free? Who was the victim, and what town or city did the crime occur?"

"We should go back and re-check hospital records from the emergency room to anyone who was admitted due to an attack?" Fisher: "Great idea Amy. We may have missed something. I'm going to ask the Captain if the chief will allow us another detective to work with us on this case for at least two days, just so we can go through hospital and court related records."

"Mike, what are you doing in the kitchen?"

"Do you want some ice tea Amy?"

"I'll try a bottle of Blue Hawaiian Cooler Mike."

"Are you serious Amy?"

"Yes Mike, I really prefer the cooler if that's okay?"

"I'll join you Amy. Do you want a glass?"

"Is the cooler nice and cold?"

"Yes it is Amy."

"Thank you Mike for the cooler and I'll use a glass."

"Did you find anything?"

"No Mike."

"Do you think the victims strapped the girls up in bondage? "I wonder about that Mike."

"Do you think that these male victims at the time got a free pass from Judge Roy Sims? According to an article I just found Mike, parents were outraged and wanted the Judge removed from the bench, and one family relocated after receiving death threats for being the first to file charges on behalf of their daughter. The names of the girls were not listed because they were the victims; probably minors and I bet you that two of the boys are now in autopsy."

"We might have a third, this kid Miller is not stable yet. We'll Amy, that's a hell of a lot of information in 20 minutes. I wonder if this one family went through the U.S. Marshall's Witness Protection Program." One girl grew up and is getting even."

"Amy, do you want to use the other room or do you need me to drive you home?"

"Do you have a robe or pajamas I could use, and maybe even another toothbrush?"

"I have pajamas I never wore and new toothbrushes. You should use the guest room since I think the double bed is better." After putting the pajamas on and brushing her teeth, Amy walks over to her partner and kisses him. Mike was pleasantly surprised. "Mike, thanks for being patient with me. You've respected my feelings, my wishes, and my beliefs. I'm in love with you Mike."

"I've fallen in love with you Amy and don't want to risk that by rushing you."

"That's just another reason why I'm in love with you. I want to wait awhile."

"So Amy, we'll spend more time together and get to know each other. Maybe we can do a picnic at the beach sometime?"

"Do you eat breakfast Mike?"

"Yes I do Amy." "What do you like to have for breakfast?"

"When I'm not in a hurry, I like to cook or go out for eggs and toast. Sometimes I buy lox, bagels, and cream cheese, toast the bagel, and add a slice of tomato with a cup of coffee and that's a treat."

"I like bagels, lox, cream cheese and coffee too."

"It's getting late Amy. We can have breakfast here in the morning, contact the U.S. Marshals tomorrow and see if we can interview people."

"Goodnight Mike."

"Good night Amy, see you in the morning."

Monday morning at 7:00 AM when Goldstein's cell phone alarm rings, she wakes up to the smell of coffee brewing and eggs over-easy prepared by Mike her partner, mentor, and the man she has fallen in love with. "I was just about to wake you Amy, breakfast is ready. Have you ever had Kona Coffee?"

"I don't think so."

"Why don't we have some breakfast and then I'll take you home so that you can change into something different from yesterday and then we continue our investigation."

"Thank you."

"You're welcome Amy. We have a full day ahead of us." Goldstein "Great coffee Mike. This even beats Starbucks Coffee and you know how much I love their coffee. You usually don't make coffee this good Mike"

"Let's rinse off the dishes, and drive over to your home where you can take a quick shower, put on a fresh outfit for work, so we can follow up on some leads, and possibly interview neighbors of the Weston's in Ventnor." Thanks Mike."

"That's a really nice television. That's a 42" Phillips."

Fisher also discovers photos of his partner with her sister and brothers when they were little kids. While standing and looking at the photos in Amy's home, Fisher sees out the corner of his eye what appears to be a cappuccino and espresso maker in the Kitchen. Next to this coffee maker is a popcorn maker, and an older one at that. "Amy, I didn't know you liked espresso or cappuccino?"

"I like cappuccino now and then but; I hardly ever use that thing. It was a gift. When I want a cappuccino, I get one at Starbucks."

"Do you own this house Amy?" Goldstein, "Yes I got a great deal. The former owners were older people who wanted to move to Florida or the Carolinas. Did I ever show you what's right outside my living room?"

"No you haven't."

"Let me show you. I enjoy having this after a rough day or week of work." Detective Goldstein opens the blinds and there is her hot tub with mini tables that can be used to hold cups or glassware, and its similar to the one her partner has. Detective Goldstein also shows: Detective Fisher how she can move the flat screen television so that it can be viewed while sitting in the hot tub from an angle. "Let me show you what I bought some months ago. It's in the garage Mike."

"What did you buy Amy, a corvette?"

"No Mike, I don't need one of them. They are not very practical. They're worthless in bad weather and nothing special."

"You have another sport utility vehicle?"

"It is an automobile but not a sports car. She opens the door to the garage where there is a specially painted fire engine red Cadillac SRX. I ordered this special. "You're one of the only ladies I know who is into automobiles. Well Amy, we need to interview people in the neighborhood where the Weston's live, contact the Marshall Service regarding the relocation of the one girl who was tied up in bondage, and is the case file sealed? If the case is sealed, then we won't be able to get the names of the girls."

"I think calling the U.S. Marshall's Service is a waste of time."

"So you want to head over to Ventnor now?"

"Yes Amy, even if a lot of people work during the day, there are people who work nights, others who do shift work, work at home, or look after their children. We both know how important it is to interview people right after a death, accident, or any incident."

"I know Mike, when information is still fresh in the minds of possible witnesses."

"You got that right."

The two detectives return to the neighborhood where the Weston's live. "Let's knock on the door to the right of the Weston's." that's closer to where the remains of Joe Tapper were found. I also want to ask the owners or owner if we can look around the backyard for possible evidence."

The detectives walk up to the front door and Fisher pushes the doorbell. "There's no answer Amy, so let's walk around to the backyard. Good, no sign of any dogs large or small. Let's look around the area close to where the remains of Mr. Tapper were found. Amy lets look around this area for a little while."

"Shouldn't we have a warrant Mike?"

"If we were looking for evidence to prove that someone in this household might be involved, then I'd make sure I'd have a warrant before even coming here."

"I didn't know that we could search without a warrant?"

"You think we should wait and come back with a warrant don't you?"

"Well Mike, I'm worried that we'll find something, and the evidence won't be admitted in court because we don't have a warrant."

"Well Amy, take a look at this."

"Is that hair?"

"It's light brown to blond hair, and I bet it belongs to someone with a traditional hair style."

"I have an envelope for that Mike."

"Thank you Amy. You see we may have found some evidence."

"I hope it doesn't belong to the neighbor or their child."

"Think positive Amy. You're too intelligent to look at things that way."

"I don't think I'm being negative here Mike, it's more like what could happen if the evidence belongs to someone who lives in this house. That's what I'm worried about Mike."

"That's okay Amy I don't see anything else we can use here. At least if it rains we may have made some progress."

"How do you know it doesn't belong to someone who lives here?"

"Were about to find out Amy. There's a car pulling into the driveway. "Are you one of the owners?" Marlene Cooper, "Yes I'm one of the owners, and these are two of our children. My husband is still at work." I'm Detective Goldstein and my partner is Detective Fisher. We are with the Egg Harbor Twp. Police Department. Can we talk with you for awhile?"

Brian, an 8 year old asks the two police detectives "Are you here because of the death of that nice guy Sunday morning?"

"May I ask a question of your son?" Mrs. Cooper, "You can ask my son questions."

"Brian, what can you tell me about the nice guy who died?"

"That guy was really nice. Joe and Rob taught me how I can throw a Frisbee and not have it go rolling on the ground rather then flying. Joe also taught me how to unlock a computer, and what I can do to develop video games. Before you can develop any computer game, you need to learn how to setup perimeters and Joe taught me the basics. Real early Sunday morning I heard noises outside and saw a woman with Joe. She was sitting on top of his waist area with a robe on. She had long light brown hair and she was shorter then Joe. When they rolled over a little, the girl took this thing that looked like a needle and that's the last thing I saw before they moved out of sight."

"Did you see her face Brian?" Brian, "I can't remember right now. I'm going to miss Joe."

"Thank you Mrs. Cooper. I'd like to give you a card in case Brian remembers anything else, you can reach us at this phone number." Mrs. Cooper, "Thank you Detectives for being so patient with Brian, the both of you have been so professional."

"Has it been more breezy around here lately?" Mrs. Cooper, "Actually it has been more breezy lately, but we figured that the weather report on the news that its going to rain."

"Thank you Mrs. Cooper and, thank you Brian. What is your name young lady? My name is Sarah. How old are you Sarah?" Sarah, "I'm 6 years old. You're a pretty girl Sarah."

The two detectives leave and walk over to the house located on the other side of the Weston home. "Let's see if anyone is home. I'll ring the door-bell a couple of times."

"I hear someone walking. The door opens and it's a woman named Sharon Blum. She's 28 years old and a fairly attractive brunette with dark brown medium length hair, brown eyes and thin build. Are you one of the owners?" Blum, "Yes I am. Who are you?"

"Were Detectives Fisher and Goldstein, I'm Amy Goldstein, and my partner Mike Fisher. Can we talk with you for a short time?" Blum, "Please come in. You're here to ask questions regarding Joe's death, aren't you?"

"That's correct Mrs. Blum. Is your husband here?"

"My husband's on his way back from Washington D.C."

"May I ask what your husband does?" Blum, "My husband's an attorney. He was in D.C. to argue a case in front of the Supreme Court because one of his client's was denied their rights under the Fifth, Sixth, and Fourteenth Amendments. I believe he's going to win this case. Our country is turning into a second rate, Communist style government."

"I'm sorry Mrs. Blum, but we need to ask you questions regarding Joe Tapper. Do you know if he had any enemies?"

"I thought about that for the past couple of years. He was acting strange detectives."

"In what way was he acting strange?" Blum, "Like someone was following him, and that he had done something wrong. I know that Joe and my husband Frank talked over some concerns that Joe had. You would have to speak to Frank about that."

"Have you seen a young female with long hair next door recently?"

"Come to think of it Detectives, I did. She was cute, petite, and had light brown hair."

"That's all you can think of right now? Could you work with a sketch artist to help us with this case?"

"Would they be willing to come to my home?"

"I think we can work that out."

"I'll be glad to assist you with your case detectives. In case Rob and Lynne from next door didn't tell you, we grew up together in the same neighborhood. Joe was a good guy for most of our childhood. He did have a dark side and seemed to get hyper when he saw or met women who were petite to medium build. He liked girls that were younger but they had to be at least 21 years old. I believe: something happened between Joe and the young girl. I think he got rough with her, she got away from him, and he was nervous since then. I think he spent the weekend with her a few years back, and it ended badly."

"Are you saying that Joe liked to role play and at times, this role playing got rough?"

"You got it. Here's something you should look for, Joe usually had girls sign a paper that said they agreed to having sex with him."

"I don't think it's necessary to know that much. You said that Joe had girls sign a paper like a contract? Where would Joe have kept these agreements?"

"You might want to ask his cousin Diane Becker that question?"

"How can we find her?"

"Diane has a Flower and gift shop near Wendy's in Northfield and yes, I'll get you the address for the shop." A few minutes later, Mrs. Blum gives a piece of paper with the name, Diane's Flower & Gift Shop (fictional) with the address and phone number on it.

Goldstein and Fisher leave the Blum residence. After getting into a Chevy Impala Fisher had signed for earlier that morning, Goldstein uses her cell phone "Is Diane Becker there? Employee Carly Barlow, "Ms. Becker should be in around 11:00 AM."

The two detectives drive over to the area where Ms. Becker's store is located and grab a cup of coffee at WAWA on Tilton Road in Northfield.

It's 10:50 AM Fisher, "I have a bad feeling about something Amy and want to drive over to Ms. Becker's store early."

The two detectives arrive at the flower and gift shop. They walk into the store where a white man with a baseball cap is trying to hold the female employee with one arm while trying to get the register terminal open with his other hand not seeing the two detectives walk in the store and approach him. Goldstein and Fisher have guns drawn on the suspect, and he still doesn't see them. "Were police officers, put your hands behind your head." The robbery suspect ignores Detective Fisher and from behind the robbery suspect, Detective Fisher slams the suspect's head into top of the register terminal and puts handcuffs on him. "I'm Detective Goldstein from the Egg Harbor Township Police Department calling to report an attempted robbery at Becker's Flower & Gift Shop on Tilton Road next door to Wendy's Hamburger's, we need officers to take this thief into custody." Sergeant Donnelly, "I'm sending officers there now." Shortly after the Northfield Police arrived and placed the suspect under arrest and using they're handcuffs, the owner of the store Diane Becker walked into her store to see police and her employee shaking like a leaf, Becker, "What happened, Carly?" Carly "That dirt bag tried to rob the store and had threatened to rape me if I didn't cooperate with him. I've seen him somewhere before but can't place where. I need time to think."

"It's best to try and remember when things are fresh in your mind." Carly, "I just can't think straight right now." Becker, "Can you give her a couple of days? Carly's just been through a bad experience."

"Do your cameras work Ms. Becker? The police can use them to prosecute that scum bag."

"Yes they do."

"You should have a sign up on that door that states you have video and audio security. It's a good idea."

"Can we ask you some questions?"

"Okay, what do you need to ask me about?"

"Do you know why Joe Tapper was acting so strange shortly before his death?"

"When Joe wasn't busy either designing new software for video games, repairing, restoring, building super-computers, teaching kids about computers, he liked role playing with girls that are of legal age, but one girl wanted him to stop midway through after teasing him for so long. She tricked him by saying that she wanted to put a new diaphragm in to prevent her from becoming pregnant. From what Joe had told me, this girl had told him that her folks would flip out on her and want him dead for getting her pregnant."

"Did you ever see her or did Joe ever tell you things about this girl."

"Joe told me she was really cute. He couldn't get her out of his mind. He even approached her at a store not so long ago and apologized to her. He came here one day and gave me $40.00 for a small basket of flowers for this girl. He told me that he apologized to her in case she felt that he hurt her, and then gave her the basket of flowers. I didn't believe him when he told me that the girl cried, hugged, and then kissed him."

"Why didn't you believe him?"

"How many girls do you know would hug someone, much less kiss someone who upset them?"

"Not too many girls I know unless, the girl has psychological problems."

"You know, I remember Joe telling me that one girl told him that she was born at least one month pre-maturely." Do you remember if he ever shared names of any girls with you?"

"No I don't."

"We heard that Joe had girls sign a paper or agreement to have consensual sex, is that true?"

"Not only is that true, he put the agreements in a fire proof security box and those agreements are at his folks place."

"Aren't his parents your Aunt and uncle?"

"Yes they are. My mother's sister stayed with her idiot second husband even after he cheated on my aunt."

"That really upset Joe. He was trying to find someone he could settle down with that of course was younger then himself."

"That's the way you described the activities of Joe Tapper."

"Joe was a nice looking guy who never had to force any woman to spend the night with him. If he wanted to, Joe could have offered any girl hundreds of dollars to spend the night with him and still not make them feel as though they were selling themselves. For Joe, the role playing was just for fun and not to hurt anyone."

"Obviously someone isn't looking at things the way you do Ms. Becker. Wasn't he your cousin?"

"He wasn't my cousin by blood."

"You're saying that you were a cousin to him as a result of a second marriage."

"That is true Detective Goldstein. I guess I didn't explain myself more clearly."

"You were very close with Joe, weren't you?"

"Yes, Detective Fisher, Joe and I were close."

"You had a romantic relationship with him, didn't you?"

"I wouldn't say it was romantic detectives. The reason why I loved Joe and more distraught then you can ever know, is because he and I were able to experience an alternative style relationship."

"What, bondage Ms. Becker?"

"No Detective Fisher, there was more to it then just bondage, as strange as that might seem. We weren't really cousins at all. Not blood relatives."

"Did Joe have photos of the girls he spent time with?"

"I believe some girls were into having photos of them-selves taken with Joe but not what you think."

"Where would he keep the photos?" Becker "In a box; under the bed where he slept prior to moving out of his folks place. This way, if one of the girls wanted to see what photos he kept, they would have to ask him. Joe would never use the photos to hurt them."

"Thank you for your help Ms. Becker."

"Can we get the address where Joe grew up?"

"Joe grew up at 4212 Walnut Avenue in Pomona, NJ near Stockton College. Let me call his parents and let them know that you want to meet with them."

Ms. Becker picks up the phone and calls Joe's parents. "Hi Aunt Sharon, "I have two detectives here from the Egg Harbor Police Department who would like to meet with you and Mark. They are trying to put a profile together of the person responsible for Joe's death. Can you meet with them now? They can come to your house within the next fifteen to twenty minutes, is that okay?" The two detectives leave the store and drive to the residence of Sharon and Mark Tapper. When they arrive at their home, Sharon Tapper is sitting on a wicker chair with a blue cushion and a cup of coffee in her right hand. "Are you Sharon Tapper?" Mrs. Tapper, "Yes I am, are you the detectives I was just informed of that were coming to see me?"

"Yes we are Mrs. Tapper, I'm Detective Amy Goldstein and this gentleman is Detective Mike Fisher. We are here to learn more about your son Joe. Were sorry for your loss and want to catch the person responsible." Mrs. Tapper, "Thank you for your kind words Detectives. I'm more then willing to assist you. I understand that two other males might also be victims at the hands of the same person."

"We don't know that yet Mrs. Tapper, but w are going to do everything we can to catch this person." Mrs. Tapper takes the two detectives to the room where her son slept, studied, and kept his belongings. "You're welcome to go through Joe's stuff and hope that it helps you catch the person who did this."

"Thank you Mrs. Tapper. We'll take care not to make a mess."

The two detectives go through the closet, the desk of the deceased, his dresser, and under the bed they find two cardboard boxes and one metal security lock box. Inside the first cardboard box, "Look what I found Amy, old collector baseball cards, and buttons from political campaigns dating back to the 1920s. Mr. Tapper even saved silver and gold collector's coins. Inside the second cardboard box, and look what I found here Amy, photos of some girls tied up but not all. "Mike, I found some DVDs and what seems like reels of film in tin cans." The two detectives can't believe how many DVDs, and photos there are, along with the reels of film.

What the two detectives also needed to assist in developing a profile would be the signed agreements that they were told should be in a security box. "I wonder if this is the security box we were informed of? Could the metal box they just found be the one?"

"What are you looking for Mike?" I'm looking for a key in the desk where the decease used to keep many of his personal items." Fisher goes through all the desk drawers and then finds a small key that he uses to Open the metal security box. Goldstein "Are those papers the agreements signed by the girls who agreed to being tied up, and making love with the deceased?"

"Yes Amy, I Not only found signed agreements but I think these other women were into the same lifestyle and our suspect was lied to and taken advantage of."

"Amy, are you saying that our suspect was a victim of bondage and other sexual acts in different locations by different people?"

"That's what I was thinking Mike, but just couldn't seem to come up with the right words."

"I know that feeling Amy."

"Mike, do you think we have enough information here to begin developing a profile of our suspect?"

"Amy, we have these photos, we have signed agreements from various young women, and the amount of agreements doesn't seem to match how many photos we have, so, I want to search a little more. Maybe look behind some of the pictures in this room. Could there be more agreements and photos in the basement if there is one, or in the garage? Did the deceased have a storage unit in the area?"

"Mrs. Tapper, did your son have a storage unit somewhere? Didn't he have his own place, and if so, where did Joe live?"

"Joe wouldn't pay for a storage unit because he didn't like the people who worked there. If Joe wanted to keep things, he would either hide them at his place, our other son or daughter's place. The stuff you found in his room upstairs is probably four or six years old, and he didn't have the opportunity to take to his place."

"Where did Joe live?" Mrs. Tapper, "Joe lived at 9614 Atlantic Avenue, I believe in Margate."

"Ms. Becker said that Joe worked on computers, designed software, and built super-computers. Do you know if Joe had any unsatisfied customers that might be angry with him?" Mrs. Tapper, "Joe wasn't perfect, no one is, but he was good with his customers, he never got into fist fights with people, he didn't beat up on women, and as far as I know, he didn't do drugs."

"Would Joe have left any personal items in the garage or basement?" Mrs. Tapper, "The only items we keep in the basement are glassware and holiday decorations. Your welcome to look around the garage."

"Thank you Mrs. Tapper. We like to take a look in the garage, and then we'll be leaving."

"Have you found anything Mike?"

"Amy, Mrs. Tapper was telling us the truth."

"Then I guess were done here."

"Thank you for your cooperation Mrs. Tapper."

"I have the victim's address in my notes? "His mother was more than cooperative with us Mike."

"Amy, some people lie while others are decent, especially when it has to do with loved ones and their memories of loved ones. "Now we go back to the office Amy and put the photos of the victim(s) on the board. What I'd like you to do, is to contact the DMV and see if we can get some help matching some, if not all the girls with their driver's licenses. While your doing that, I'm going to contact a friend of mine at the FBI in Trenton and see if we can get some cooperation from the U.S. Marshall's Office regarding their witness protection program." While the two detectives are driving back to their office, they get stuck in traffic due to an automobile accident. "I'm going to use my laptop to get into the database for the New Jersey Department of Motor Vehicles. "Did you hack security?"

"I learned a lot from playing around with computers and watching a former partner I worked with. He was able to get into the system the CIA or even the FBI use."

"You could end up in serious trouble Amy for hacking into a state or federal computer system."

"Don't worry Mike, the captain and chief won't let that happen."

"I hope your right Amy I relish the thought of having to break in a new partner."

"Are you worried about me Mike?" Detective Fisher looks over at his partner and tells her, "Yes Amy, I am worried that you will get in trouble for this, and I'll lose you."

"Don't worry Mike you won't lose me just because I hacked into the data base for the DMV." Shortly after hacking into the DMV's computer, Detective Goldstein finds photo licenses that match two of the women found in the box owned by the deceased Joe Tapper. "What did you find Amy?"

"I found two photo licenses that match two girls in photos that were under the bed where Joe Tapper grew up. I can't believe that Mr. Tapper didn't take more care in protecting the photos."

"In my opinion Amy, Mr. Tapper did take steps to protect the photos. He put the photos in a box not clearly labeled and at his parents place, making it almost impossible for anyone to find them. The question is, what photo if any, is that of our killer?"

"I wonder if there are any photos of the girl who is responsible for these homicides."

"What do you mean Amy?"

"Think about it Mike. If you thought there was the possibility of any photos of you in bondage, would you take the lives of those who photographed you, making it easier for the police to catch you based on of course motive?"

"Amy, first, I'm not a young lady; and it's difficult for me to look at things that way. Also, our suspect is allowing their anger to get the best of them. Did you ever see the Godfather Part III?"

"No Mike."

"In the movie, the lead character Michael Corleone, tells his nephew Vincent that you "Never hate your enemies, it affects your judgment." Even though it was used in a Godfather movie, it makes sense in real life, doesn't it?"

"Mike It doesn't mean that we'll catch our suspect before she takes another life. The person who killed these guys might have already left the state."

"Well Amy, maybe we should check ticket sales for flights out of AC Intl Airport for the past couple of days?"

"Mike, I was just thinking out loud."

"You do that a lot, don't you?"

"Yes Mike, I do that a lot. You haven't seen what I'm like when I have a suspect sitting or standing in front of me."

"So Amy, you really think that our suspect may have left the state?"

"Yes Mike, I think our suspect could have left the state."

"How many photo licenses have you been able to match up?"

"I've matched up four photos, agreements signed, with photo licenses. Not bad Mike." Fisher, "As long as you don't get in any trouble for this

Amy. Do you know how many people have gotten in serious trouble for hacking into the computer systems of government agencies?"

"I know about that Mike. We are law enforcement officers trying to find someone who killed two people, and our captain knows that I will use any method necessary to solve crimes as long as they are legal. "Have you found anymore photos of girls, their agreements that match up with driver's licenses?"

"No Mike, I've only found the four that matched up. What I'd like to do is involve the news media like some police departments and victims of families ask for help. Maybe we could contact John Walsh of The Hunt?"

"That's a good idea Amy."

"Do you think the idea of using The Hunt and other media is taking the easy way?"

"No Amy, I think it's an excellent idea. Maybe we'll get some good leads with the help of the media."

"We'll clear it with the captain when we get back to the office."

"I'm changing the subject Amy, but what are you doing for dinner?"

"I'm getting together with my mother, aunt, and my grandmother."

The two detectives return to their office and its Wednesday afternoon. When they arrive, none of the other detectives are in the office. When Fisher looks into the captain's office, he's in there with the chief. The captain and chief are talking quietly when Fisher knocks on the door. Captain Costello "Come in Mike." Detective Fisher walks into Captain Costello's office and closes the door behind him. Chief Braun, "Mike, have you and Amy learned anything new other then Amy hacking into the DMV system, with a smile on his face."

"Yes Chief Braun, Amy was able to match up photos of women that were taken while they were tied up, with their signed agreements including for consensual sex. So far, Amy and I don't believe that we found a photo of our suspect." The Chief, "Have you asked for any help from the State Police?"

"No we haven't Chief. I did have plans to call the U.S. Marshall's Service since one of the girls' who was tied up and testified, was relocated along with her family. Amy thinks it's a waste of our time. Mr. Tapper wasn't the one brought into court. Although, I don't believe Mr. Tapper was the one who tied the one girl up in bondage who testified, I do believe that he had knowledge or was friends with those who did. I won't be surprised if the Marshal Service refuses to cooperate." The Chief, "I don't believe the Marshal's Service will help up us Mike." Costello, "How's Amy doing?"

"Amy's doing real good. She had me worried when she went on the computer in the car and got into the DMV database using a stick that she plugged into a USB port. Amy's obviously done this before." The Chief, "Amy's able to get into the computer systems of government agencies and even the FBI hasn't come down on her. I'm afraid Amy will go too far someday and we won't be able to help her."

"Keep an eye on her Mike. "Don't worry Captain. Do you want me to have a talk with Amy regarding her breaking into agency computer systems?"

"If you do say anything to Amy: make sure she realizes that we don't want her to get into trouble with the FBI." Chief Braun, "Amy is becoming a real "Cracker Jack" detective isn't she Lou?"

"Amy and I came up with the idea of contacting The Hunt to assist us with this investigation.

Would you and the Chief agree with us doing so?" Captain, "I like the idea, what about you Chief?" Chief Braun, I'm not sure if I want the public to know. Let's keep this investigation confidential."

"I'll let Amy know."

"Are you going to interview more people?"

"I think Amy and I should fall back a little and work on a plan to catch this young lady." Captain Costello, "What would you do if it turned out to be a guy?"

"Why would you think it might be a guy?"

"How do you know if this guy Tapper had other ideas? He may have been making films that featured alternate life styles or films for swingers?"

"You think Amy and I need to interview more people who knew the deceased?"

"Yes Mike, you need to interview more people.

At 4:00 PM Amy walks into the office with bags of Chinese food from The China Bowl in Egg Harbor Twp. near what is left of the Mays Landing Mall before a lot of stores closed due to the poor economy. In the delivery bags there is Chinese food for Detectives Goldstein, Pamela. After taking two orders of Sweet and Sour Chicken down to the lab, Detective Goldstein sits down with Fisher and her direct supervisor Captain Costello to discuss the investigation. Captain Costello, "Mike told me that you came up with the idea of asking the public for help by contacting The Hunt. That's a great idea Amy but the chief doesn't like the idea."

"Captain, that was an idea that both of us came up with. If the police department were to share some ideas with the public on "The Hunt" maybe someone will call in with a name of someone or clear description."

"Chief Braun is against the idea regarding this case okay. "It's a shame the chief is against the idea so we'll drop it for now."

"The biggest problem we have is a description of our suspect from a child. The young boy did tell us that our un-sub has light brown hair and that her hair is long which matches the hair sample we found. We know that she is thin and that's it so far.

I remember what that little boy said Mike, but we can't base the description of our suspect on the words of a little boy alone."

While finishing their dinner the phone rings, and Fisher grabs the phone allowing Captain Costello to continue eating. Beth Stein, "I'd like to speak to Detective Fisher or Goldstein, this is Beth Stein."

"Hello Ms. Stein, this is Detective Fisher, how can I help you?" Ms. Stein, "Detective Fisher I saw a young lady who was petite, light brown hair that is traditionally long." She has blue eyes, and she is so innocent looking. Detective Fisher, "What direction was she walking or driving toward, and if driving what kind of automobile and color is it?"

"She's not driving she is walking up to the field near my home and where I found the young male on the incline to the field."

"Was she carrying anything?"

"I didn't see anything in her hands. She's wearing jeans and I believe a green top."

"Did you see what kind of car she was driving or got out of?"

"No I didn't. Do you think I should try to strike up a conversation with her?"

"No Ms. Stein. Just try to keep an eye on her without making her nervous or that she doesn't see you looking in her direction." Ms. Stein, "Thank you Detective Fisher. Are you on your way here?"

"My partner and I just got in the car and we should be there in ten minutes or so." Seven minutes later detectives Fisher and Goldstein pull up in front of the home belonging to Beth Stein. Fisher, "Hello Ms. Stein, do you know if the young lady is still in the field?" Ms. Stein, "I think she left in a Japanese made car?"

"Was it a Honda or Toyota?"

"No detectives, I don't believe it was either make. It might have been a wagon but I'm not really sure it's dark out now. I can tell you the car wasn't white or silver."

"Thank you Ms. Stein."

The two detectives leave the property of Ms. Stein and walk over to the field. When they get to the field Detective Goldstein finds a foot but no heel print. "I bet she was wearing sneakers. "Why would this young lady come back to the field where she killed someone?" Fisher, "Maybe she lost something and thought it might still be there like an earring or maybe a cell phone or pair of glasses?"

"Let's look around for awhile Amy. We don't need to rush back to the office. I'll have to let the captain know we are looking for some evidence. Amy, we need to continue asking ourselves why this person has committed these crimes and how. "Maybe our suspect has been following her victims?"

"I thought we discussed this before Amy?"

"While we are here at the location of the first victim I think it's a good idea to go back to the beginning. Let's try to use the same tools FBI Profilers use that are with the Behavior Analysis Unit. Has our suspect had a psychotic break as a result of reliving a traumatic experience?"

"If this young lady has done so, then we need to get her some help." Captain Costello, "I'm calling you Mike because in my experience dealing with a serial killer, there are two things that could happen, the first being that our suspect can suddenly stop, in which case it becomes impossible for us to the catch them, or we could have a serial killer who will never stop unless we catch them. We shouldn't wait any longer and ask for FBI agents from the Behavior Analysis Unit to assist us."

"I tried putting a couple calls into the FBI office but no response yet. Someone at the FBI office in Trenton said they would get back to me by tomorrow. Let's wait until 2:00 PM tomorrow and if we don't hear from anyone, I'll call Lenny Wolf.

Its 7:00 PM and the September evening is getting cooler. Fisher and Goldstein didn't find anything where the first victim was discovered. They left the area and went back to the office. A short time after retuning to the office, the phone rings in the violent crime and homicide unit. Captain Costello takes the call from his friend and Special Agent Lenny Wolf from the FBI. "Hello Lenny how's the family?" Agent Wolf "The family is good Lou, how's yours' doing?"

"One of my little girls is getting married soon. Do you remember Jennifer?"

"I remember when she was just 10 years old Lou."

"Karen and I did send your family an invitation, you didn't get it?"

"I'll ask Ellen, she's better at keeping track of the mail."

"Spoken like a true man as Karen would say."

"How is Karen doing Lou, is she better since she is off the medication after suffering the traumatic brain injury?"

"Karen is doing a lot better Lenny, thanks for your concern. Lenny, can you help us with a serious case?" Agent Wolf, "Is this about the two murders and the one young male found in the backyard of his family's home?"

"That's the case Lenny but that young man is still alive."

"We use a template we call victimology. This is the study of a victim and a way for authorities to narrow a list of probable types of suspects. Learn what type of life styles the victims lived? I'll tell you what my friend, if you can have the detectives who have been working on this case put all their notes together, then we'll put together a profile of your suspect. It sounds like your un-sub is out for revenge and that means they could have had a psychotic break. They are delusional, had a break with reality."

"Lenny, there were two young males found dead with similar wounds and we have a New Jersey State Trooper guarding another young male. I'm thinking a few possibilities here. First, he really wasn't a target but only used to throw us off while our suspect plans to kill another victim, second, our suspect may have heard someone walking around and they took off in fear of getting caught, or our suspect really liked this young male but still wanted to hurt him for hurting her. Maybe our suspect had a list and is finished?"

"That's always a possibility Lou, and there have been people who stop assaulting or killing people but only for a matter of time, and then start again. Serial killers usually know what they're doing is wrong but don't give themselves up. Ted Bundy is a perfect example of that. Not that the murders Ted Bundy committed have anything to do with this case but, the point I was trying to make was that most serial killers don't quit and don't give themselves up. How do you think our suspect is able to commit these crimes without leaving a finger or footprint?"

"Both detectives working on this case in addition to our coroner have not been able to determine what this suspect is using to avoid detection. We considered latex gloves, fabric, and leather."

"We could be looking at a new product that was recently developed for medical use. Tell your detectives to meet with managers or owners of medical supply companies. Have your detectives ask if there are new products someone could use to protect their identity. When your detectives are finished asking questions, they should have answers either yes, and what the product is, or no, there is no such product and need to keep looking."

"Thanks Lenny, I'll get back to you as soon as we learn something."

"You have my cell number in case you need it Lou?"

"I sure do Lenny." Captain, "I'm not like many captains, I'll interview suspects or bystanders just like I expect my detectives to do. One thing I don't do is get angry so detectives under my command learn how to interrogate a suspect."

"Lou, I take my job seriously and sometimes I'm told that I'm too laid back but my superiors do know they can count on me to follow regulations."

"Have a good evening Lenny."

"You too Lou."

It's Thursday morning when Goldstein's phone rings and Detective Fisher is the one calling her at 6:30 AM? "Hello, who's calling so early?"

"Come on Amy, its Mike. I found a medical supply center and we are going to meet with the owner Henry Kruger in two hours. So get ready, I'm taking you out for breakfast."

"Can you give me a half hour Mike?"

"I'll pick you up at 7:15. See you then Amy." Forty-five minutes later and there is the sound of a horn. It's Mike Fisher and he is already drinking a cup of coffee he picked up at WAWA. I got you a cup of coffee too Amy."

"Thank you for the coffee Mike, and just the way I like it. "Let's go for breakfast." After breakfast at the Shore Diner Mike tells Amy, "The owner of the medical supply center will help us."

"I hope your right Mike. We can use a break on this case."

"Are you having doubts that we'll solve this case Amy? "Even if we get help from the FBI would that matter? The important thing is to stop our suspect from doing anymore harm or killing another person. I'd be more then willing to work with the FBI." Fisher "Good Amy: because the Captain spoke to the director of the FBI Field office in Trenton. Lenny Wolf is going to assist us. He is great at profiling people. Agent Wolf believes that if there are no finger or footprints and all we found are marks from a syringe, he suggested talking with managers or owners of medical supply stores who would know of new products on the market similar to latex gloves."

The detectives arrive at the Medical Supply Store where they meet with the owner Henry Kruger. "Mr. Kruger, we are Detectives Fisher and Goldstein." Kruger, "Please to meet you; and what is it that I can do to assist you?"

"We have two male victims and one recovering in a hospital. Our suspect has been able to commit these crimes without leaving a single finger or footprint." Is there a new kind of latex or cloth that enables someone not to leave any prints behind?"

"Although latex doesn't necessarily leave a finger or footprint on the outside of the glove, a person probably does leave their fingerprint on the inside of the glove. I don't know of any medical supplies that fit over the feet other then the color socks you might be issued while in a hospital to keep your feet warm."

"Take a look at this Mike, a mask like the one used in the play Phantom of the Opera. Where did you get it?" I purchased it for my son on the Internet. He played the Phantom and he's only 14 years old."

"What are these made of?"

"I'm really not sure Detective Goldstein. It could be made of some form of plastic or rubber."

"If this is made to be so flexible that a person can wear it on their face to perform in front of thousands of people and it doesn't fall apart, then what about the same material being molded to a person's hand, not latex, rubber, or plastic."

"Wait a minute; do any of you remember Mission Impossible?" In both the television series and movies, molds were made to fit over the faces of the actors to appear as someone else? If that could be done as you just brought up Amy with regards to the Phantom of the Opera, then why not gloves?"

"I'm just beginning to realize what the two of you have been asking. Sorry about that, got a lot on my mind lately. I want to show both of you something but you have to keep quiet about this. Not to get political here, but I believe the politicians in Washington don't want senior citizens with arthritis to know these machines exist. As far as the public should know, this machine is for people who suffer from work related injuries, and not for use by senior citizens."

"What does this machine actually do?"

"This medical device makes a mold that fits to a hand. You might even say when someone is wearing this glove, they are wearing a Paraffin Glove." Fisher's cell phone begins to ring "God bless America,"

"Excuse me I don't want to be rude sir, but I have to take this call. Hello Captain, Amy and I have been talking to the owner of this medical supply store and his assistance has proven more helpful then even Mr. Kruger realizes." The phone rings again and Detective Fisher answers, "Who is this?"

"Mike, this is Helen Ross your favorite coroner and forensic expert. Have I got some news for you but this still could be a long shot. I found a long strand of hair on the T-shirt of the first victim. It is light brown in color; and I was able to get some DNA from this sample. I can tell you this from the strand of hair Mike that the young lady in question, takes very good care of herself."

"Can you tell how she might keep her hair?"

"Do you mean the style of her hair?"

"Yes Helen."

"She keeps her hair straight, uses a conditioner, and can tell you that it's an Avon product."

"Thanks Helen." Goldstein, "Excuse me a moment Mr. Kruger and walks over to Detective Fisher. "Mike: who called you?"

"It was Helen who called. She found a long straight, strand of light brown hair on the T-shirt of the first victim, and was able to get a DNA sample from the hair. Did you know that forensic experts are able to determine if someone uses hair conditioner, and who makes or sells it?" Our un-sub purchased her conditioner from Avon."

"You're kidding Mike." Goldstein has a real surprised look on her face. "Thank you sir for your help today, but we have to go back to our office."

The two detectives are driving back to the department when Detective Fisher's cell phone rings again. "Amy, please take my phone."

"Hello, this is Detective Goldstein."

"This is Helen Ross Amy. Guess what I learned Amy?"

"What did you learn Helen?"

"The first two male victims were dead longer then we originally thought."

"I'm putting you on speaker Helen."

"The reason why I know it's been longer then a few hours would be the maggots on the two victims I missed before. Sorry about that. Since discovering the maggots, the time of death is now more difficult to determine but within a twenty-four hour to forty eight hour time frame since the temperature effects the time it takes for a body to decompose then you have flies."

"I've never been into biology but my guess is that the warmer the weather, the faster the body decomposes?"

"That's absolutely right Amy."

"So, our un-sub (unknown subject) had one or two hours to commit the murder and disappear without anyone seeing her. She could be a professional killer. I can't believe this girl."

"Helen, have you had the opportunity to put the DNA sample into the data base?"

"No I haven't Mike. "Telling what I know entering the sample probably won't turn up anything. This girl is really good."

"First Amy and now you Helen, it sounds like the both of you are rooting for her."

"I thought you agreed with our suspect, that if you learned the victims assaulted, or took advantage of our suspect and other young girls, you would be inclined to look the other way or get her a lighter sentence?"

"This might be true Amy but, the way you and Helen are talking about this female suspect, makes me think that you are both looking up to her."

"No Mike, we are not looking at this suspect as though she is some kind of hero but, you have to admit she has guts for going after these guys. I just wonder how many guys she has on her list to get even with, or if she is done, and then good luck in trying to catch her."

"Let's go outside for a few minutes Amy, I want to talk to you."

The two detectives walk outside the police department so that Detective Fisher can share something that is on his mind. "If it were up to me and I felt that this un-sub wasn't going to hurt innocent people, I would look the other way. I would tell this girl to pack the basics she would need to leave the state and have someone forward her other belongings later. Let's keep this between us Amy, okay?"

"Okay Mike, I trust your judgment; and know you have something on your mind you're not ready to share."

"Amy forget what I just said, can you contact Avon and see what salesperson sold conditioner in this area?"

"What are you doing after work?"

"I hadn't made any plans Amy."

"Want to have dinner at my place tonight?"

"Is it okay if I follow you after work?"

"Of course Mike. I was planning on cooking up some pasta. I bought some gourmet sauce the other day, and already cooked the meatballs."

"Do you have any red wine?"

"I might have a bottle of red wine but forget what kind of wine it is."

"Let's stop off at the liquor store near your place. You might have Merlot at home and I'm no big fan of Merlot.

It's November 1, 2010 and the two detectives have left work at 4:30 PM. It was a quiet day, but a somewhat successful day. "Amy, do you like wine that is more or less sweet?"

"I really prefer wine that's not too sweet."

"Good, then I'll buy a bottle of Cabernet Sauvignon. The problem with this wine is if you don't finish it and you put it in the refrigerator, it seems to change the taste of the wine. "Mike, Isn't that because red wine is suppose to be served at room temperature?"

"That's true Amy." What do you think about the information we learned today?"

"I don't understand how the use of a glove can allow for someone to go un-detected even when it comes to forensics?"

"This is not a typical glove Amy. This glove is more like a wax but it's not like the wax or feeling you get when handling a candle. Like you, I'm not sure how using this material that allows for someone to go un-detected. Chemistry has never been an area of interest of mine."

"It's not so much what chemicals are used Mike, it's the use of a mold and does someone have to get measured or fitted for a particular size glove, or is the mold produced to allow flexibility? Think about this Mike, when you go into a clothing store to look for a pair of gloves, there are different sizes."

"You mean small, medium, and large?"

"That's it Mike." Detective Goldstein's holding a pair of leather gloves in her hands and then "How long have you had the burgundy leather gloves for?"

"I've had these gloves for awhile."

"Put them on Amy?" That's when the two detectives begin to realize that they are on to something.

The spaghetti is cooking; "Mike, do you usually put sugar in the sauce while it's cooking?"

"Amy you're right. Put the sugar in while it's cooking so that it cuts the acid." While the sauce is heating up on the stove, the two detectives are watching the local news when they hear that a woman was seen getting into a small car and the parents of a young male are heard screaming from the backyard of their home near the Shoprite Supermarket in English Creek: "Another victim Amy. We do have a serial killer on our hands."

"Let's just have dinner and hopefully we won't get a call until tomorrow morning. Don't we deserve a quiet evening together?" Goldstein, "Mike, would you like to try a piece of cherry pie that was freshly baked at the market."

"Of course Amy, that sounds good." While her partner and mentor rinses off the dishes and places them in the dishwasher, Detective Goldstein takes the pie out of the refrigerator and puts a couple of pieces in her microwave convection oven to heat, but not until they make a couple cups of coffee first.

"I'm going to heat these pieces of pie Mike. Do you want any ice cream or whipped cream to go with your piece of pie?"

"If your having ice cream I'll join you."

"After dessert we can go over what we already have done time and again. We aren't gaining any ground with this case. Our suspect always seems to be ahead of us. This is frustrating Mike."

"I agree Amy it seems rather odd that we never discovered any footprints. What just popped in my head is that it's our suspect's hand or hands that are the mold for the gloves. When we were in the Medical Supply store, the owner was trying to tell us that the person makes they're own glove. Amy, Come check this out. Watch this there is an actual demonstration on the Internet. See what this actor is doing, they are putting their hand inside and then when they pull their hand out they have a glove on their hand or hands. They only need wax paper."

"It still doesn't explain why our un-sub never left a footprint. It's not like they are going to dip their feet in this machine." Detective Fisher is so surprised by his partner's comment that he laughs harder then he has for sometime. "Think about this Amy, maybe our suspect dragged her feet so she wouldn't leave a footprint?"

"I wonder, (with a curious look on her face), if this same woman has gone after young males in other towns or even The Philadelphia area?"

"Somehow Amy, I wouldn't jump to conclusions. We've already determined that we are looking for a young lady in her early twenties, and this is the reason for my believing that we stick to the surrounding areas."

"Okay Mike, let's concentrate on the areas where we found the victims."

"I'm with you; we are taking the rest of the night off from police related work."

"Excuse me Mike I want to change into something more comfortable."

"Are you trying to tell me something Amy?"

"I just want to be more comfortable Mike." Detective Fisher remembers when Amy was still a rookie cop. "Do you want me to open the bottle of wine?"

"Please do Mike."

"I want you to know Amy that I really love you. I hope that you are not uncomfortable with anything I'm saying to you Amy, but I want for you and us to spend the rest of our lives together. I want for you to be my wife, so Amy, will you marry me?" Goldstein, "Yes Mike, I want for us to spend the rest of our lives together. I really love you Mike. I'm not sure what to say to my family, I can almost see their faces now, and by the way, during the Christmas and holiday season Mike and I will be setting up a Christmas tree and Hanukkah bush for the holidays."

"Amy, even when the lighting is dim I can see your beauty as though it is bright in here."

It's Sunday morning 7:30 AM when the phone rings waking Goldstein and Fisher who were sleeping in separate rooms since Goldstein wants to take things slowly. "Amy, this is Captain Costello, there was another murder and this time on Thomas Jefferson Road near the Shoprite Supermarket in English Creek."

"Is the CSI team sure that it's the same un-sub?" Costello, "Yes Amy, they are sure it's the same un-sub. Have you seen Mike or heard from him since yesterday afternoon?"

"I'm sure Mike is fine, and I will tell him that we need to head to the crime scene"

"You are going to the home of Bernie and Barbara Franklin. They live at, believe it or not, 1776

Thomas Jefferson Road."

"Wow, are you serious? So, this young male is dead?"

"Just drive over there as soon as you can Amy."

Fisher is in the shower and Detective Goldstein tells him "Mike, the captain just called and we have another crime scene to go to. The address is 1776 Jefferson Road. Detective Fisher "Are you kidding?"

"No Mike, I'm not kidding."

"I'm almost dressed and we'll get some coffee on the way."

"I'm ready Mike, both side arms ready, a canister of pepper spray ready and waiting for you."

"Shaved, shoes and shirt on, do you remember where I put my coat?"

"It's on the coat rack Mike." Fisher, "Got my gun, got my coat, and ready."

"I'll set the alarm Mike. Do you want to use my car?"

"We'll use the Escape Amy." Out of the house and now in Fisher's Ford Escape, "We are going to the home of the Franklin's."

Detectives Fisher and Goldstein arrive at the Franklin home, and Detective Fisher has a strange feeling that they are being watched and maybe even a target by the un-sub. "This is what we are going to do Amy, we are going to get out of this truck from your side and stay down. If a few friends of mine listened to me years ago, it would have been a different future for two of them, and one who died at the scene. After getting out of Fisher's Ford Escape, Fisher notices a flash of sunlight due to a reflection from a metal object like a watch. Did you see the make of that car Amy?"

"No I didn't Mike. The person who was driving took off pretty fast"

Fisher looks around with caution, than he and Goldstein walk to the front door of the Franklin home and then ring the doorbell. "Look up to your left Mike."

When Fisher looks up he sees a small camera. On the intercom there is a voice asking them, Annie the housekeeper, "Can you show me your ID and badges using the camera. Seconds afterward a woman opens the door to let the detectives enter the home. The housekeeper and nanny for the Franklin family escorts Fisher and Goldstein to the dining room where Bernie, Barbara, and yes, their son Benjamin is sitting. Mrs. Franklin, "You are the two officers looking for the young lady who came to thank my son?"

"Actually Mrs. Franklin, we were told a homicide was committed." Goldstein, "What do you mean she came to thank your son?"

"Yes officers, this young lady came to our home and thanked Benjamin for helping her. Why don't you tell these officers how you helped her Ben?" Ben, "There were four guys, but only two of them wanted to rape her, and the other two wanted to watch. I told her she didn't ask for it, I told them to stop and I called 911." Detective Goldstein, "So these guys raped this girl or young lady?" Benjamin, "Yes, and because she told them she wanted to wait until she met the right guy but Joe Tapper wasn't involved."

"Do you know where this young lady is now, and what her name is?"

"I can answer detectives. Then a man walked into the dining room wearing a black hat and telling the detectives, "I am a security consultant but right now I can't tell you who I work for but the young lady is gone.

I'm Michael Thorn and its best that both of you write this case off as a "cold case."

"What would you say to the families who lost a member of their family?" Thorn, "Tell them that the young lady who may have been responsible for these acts may have taken her own life. Articles of clothing have been found on a bridge with a letter." Detective Fisher "You want us to lie, is that it?" Thorn, "Do what it takes Detectives. I will tell you this, you may meet this young lady sometime but you will never be able to charge her for the deaths of the two boys or for the injuries of the other boy. She is too valuable to our country." Thorn turns to the Franklin's son are you okay Ben." Their son shakes his head yes and replies, "Mr. Thorn, I really liked her and would do almost anything to help her."

"I know Ben I know you really care about her." Mr. Franklin, "Can I show you out officers? There isn't any reason for you to be here now. Our son is safe."

"No Mr. Franklin, we can find our way out."

After the two detectives walk outside the Franklin residence Detective Fisher, "I have a plan but you can't tell anyone. Amy lets go sit in the truck for awhile."

"What do you have in mind Mike?"

"Trust me Amy, I have a feeling that something is up, and even if we can't arrest our un-sub, I'd like to find out who she is if possible."

"What if Mr. Thorn can have us fired or worse? He gave me the impression that he can cause us a lot of problems."

"Don't worry Amy, I wouldn't be doing this if there were a serious risk that we could be fired, black balled, or killed."

Detective Fisher plugs what looks like just a black box into an AC outlet in his truck; it's a mini amp for a digital recorder and mini speakers that work with bugging devices. "What are you doing?"

"We are going to listen to their private meeting."

"Even if it's illegal we still missed a lot by now." Fisher, "No we haven't. The devices I left in their home started recording right after I planted them. This laptop computer will make it possible for us to listen to their conversation from the moment the listening devices were planted."

"We could never use the information to arrest them."

"That's not what we are after Amy, even if we can't bring her to justice in a court of law, there is the court of public opinion."

"Did I hear right, this girl is living in Egg Harbor Township?"

"Let's keep it down, and wait for it Amy."

Fisher is waiting, hoping that he and Goldstein will hear the name of their un-sub. Amy is getting cold and reaches for a blanket. Then they hear it, the un-sub's first name is Tanya and she was born in Israel not America, but came to the states with her parents when she was 5 years old. After forty minutes they hear Mr. Thorn, "I need to leave. Tomorrow's going to be a busy day for me."

"Look Amy, Thorn is leaving and we are going to follow him. I'd like to meet this girl even if we can't arrest her, just to see why she went after these guys."

"The Franklin kid wasn't going to tell us anything other than that the guys she killed raped her. The kid didn't know that two of the boys wanted to make a sex slave out of this young woman. I think there is more to this story. Don't you remember the conversation we had with the couple in Ventnor, their friend was acting suspicious like someone had been following him."

"You mean the Weston's. I remember that Amy, and wonder if that guy Joe really liked our un-sub and let her get too close after this Franklin kid helped by calling 911."

"Where do you think Thorn is going?"

"I'm hoping Mr. Thorn is going to lead us to our un-sub. I'm hoping he doesn't spot us."

"That could be a problem Mike he could call our bosses and accuse us of harassment."

"Let the scum-bag complain Amy, I'd like to find this young lady and don't care if he threatens to have us suspended."

"Where do you think he's going?"

"I hope he's going home so we can find out where Mr. Thorn lives. Then, we can follow him tomorrow." Detective Goldstein, "So Mike, we find out where Mr. Thorn lives and tail him tomorrow. Why not wait until he goes into his home and when it looks like he's gone to bed or taking a shower, we plant tracking bugs on his automobiles." Fisher, "Amy, your telling me that you have tracking devices?"

"Yes, actually Mike, I brought three with me."

"Where did you get those?"

"The department Mike: prior to us working together. You keep watch Mike, and I'll plant the bugs."

"Wait Amy, do you see that behind the tree mounted to the roof?" Detective Goldstein, "Yes Mike, that's not the only security camera. Just use this microphone and ear piece to keep me informed if there is a problem."

Detective Goldstein wearing black shoes, black slacks, and a green top moving around as though she is a trained spy for the government, attaches the tracking devices to Mr. Thorn's automobiles. He collects automobiles but he only drives two of them regularly. His blue 1963 Corvette with the top down for good weather days; and he has the Jeep Grand Cherokee Limited for long trips; when he goes fishing or skiing. Goldstein doesn't take a chance, she places a third tracking device on Mr. Thorn's Volvo Cross Country Wagon when he doesn't want to drive the Jeep. A few minutes later, Detective Goldstein jumps back into her partner's truck. "That was easy."

"I was worried about you the entire time you were out there."

"Thanks for caring Mike but I've done this before.

Detective Fisher, "What are you Amy, a female 007?"

"I wanted to bust a guy who attacked a girl I knew in school so I planted tracking devices in his pickup truck, his parents' garage, and even his bedroom." Detective Fisher, "You risked your career and your life to get someone like that, illegally?"

"Mike, it was the actions I took that led to me becoming a detective. My instincts led me to urge my captain to get me a warrant to place bugs so that we could get this guy on tape and put him away. I had a strong feeling that this guy had attacked other women who were afraid to come forward, that he was a predator." Fisher, "You handled the Kendall predator case?"

"Yes Mike."

"There he is; looks like he's getting ready for bed."

"That sounds like a good idea."

"Yes Amy, we are going to stay at that hotel across the street."

"Did you make a reservation and didn't tell me?"

"I'm calling right now." Detective Fisher even in the dead of night with vision like a cat uses his smart phone to call the Hampton Hotel. When the front desk clerk answers the phone Detective Fisher, "I made a reservation earlier to get a hotel room, my confirmation number is NT110025 and the name is Mike Gustuv (under-cover name). The hotel clerk, "Your room is ready Mr. Gustuv and there are two beds like you wanted. The two detectives pull up to the hotel and Fisher reaches for a suitcase with wheels, dark blue in color and a handle he uses to pull the case. The two detectives walk up to check in and Detective Fisher "I'm going to pay ahead of time since we might have to rush out." The hotel clerk, everyone calls Big Aaron is quite husky. Aaron, "Here's the key card but it's the same room for the two of you?" Detective Fisher, "That's right sir."

Detective Goldstein with a big grin on her face, "Everything is fine. "Amy, I think this guy has issues with us sharing a room." Goldstein, "Tell Mike why you have an issue with me sharing a room with him."

"What are you talking about?" Aaron, "So, you are Mike Fisher not Gustuv?"

"What is your problem sir?" Aaron, "I just wanted to bust your stones since you made a reservation to stay with Amy in the same hotel room. I know it has to do with your job, but Mike, Amy is my cousin and we look out for each other. Not all family members look out for one another, but we do."

"You're her cousin?" Aaron, "Again, here is your card key Mike." Goldstein grabs it. The day after attaching tracking devices, Detective Fisher, "It looks like Thorn is stopping at that rancher with the white fence and golden retriever. Fisher and Goldstein try not to stand out while doing surveillance. I need those binoculars. "I'm trying to get this digital surveillance antenna to work with the radio. Amy finally gets the antenna to work. "So far I don't hear anything that would allow me to believe that our un-sub is in the house."

"Can I listen and maybe we can learn who owns this house." Goldstein, "That sounds good to me Mike." Detective Goldstein couldn't stop laughing. "What is so funny Amy?" Goldstein, "You are Mike. You have been a detective for at least five years and still you aren't able to look up information to learn who owns this house or other properties."

"You are better at finding information then I am. You can also get away with more than I'm able to when it comes to getting into computer systems."

"You still do things the old fashioned way Mike."

"Yes Amy, if I need information on a property owner I'm more likely to go to a court house then use a computer."

"Look Amy, Mr. Thorn is coming out of the house, a place decorated contemporary style with the exception of the back of the house finished Roman style including the in-ground pool. Mr. Thorn, prior to becoming an agent of the Federal government, has also been a successful building and electrical engineer. Thorn is using his cell phone, "I'm on my way" Thorn tells someone, not telling how long it might be until I find myself in serious trouble with one of our enemies, that's the price I pay for the way I make my living. Thorn chooses to use his Jeep. "It looks like Thorn is planning to do some driving."

"Mike, do you think he's planning to go out of state, and if so, why wouldn't he have packed more clothes?" Fisher, "Maybe Thorn is taking a trip where he already has clothes available to him? Men like Thorn usually have second homes or hotels they use when they travel."

"I bet this guy Thorn has our suspect Tanya hidden. If she were anyone else they would be facing charges. It's not fair to the families of the victims."

"Most likely our suspect was a victim too."

"Do you think we'll find out today?"

"I hope so Amy. It would be nice if we could learn what happened, help the families of the victims have some closure, and we can close this case successfully while having some quiet time between cases."

"Mike, where do you think Mr. Thorn is driving?"

"I think Mr. Thorn is taking us towards Philadelphia." Just then, Mr. Thorn takes a right turn from the Black Horse Pike and then makes a left, then after a short time Mr. Thorn takes a half turn through a circle and drives towards the White Horse Pike passing the Navel Air Center: and then reaching the White Horse Pike with a WAWA on the left hand side. "Do you think Thorn spotted us Mike?"

"No I don't Amy, and we are going to continue to follow Mr. Thorn. The weather report for the day is cloudy with the chance of extreme downpours. Most drivers are using their headlights since New Jersey State law requires drivers to use their headlights if windshield wipers are used. While following Mr. Thorn Detective Fisher, "The weather is getting really bad like an extreme downpour. Look at the sky, Fisher, "There could be a tornado. Goldstein "Do you see the color of the sky?"

"Yes Amy, it's an interesting color."

"I've been to Kansas and seen one up close. The color of the sky right now is very similar to what you see when there is going to be a tornado."

"It looks as though Mr. Thorn is pulling into the shopping center where the Wendy's is."

"We have to keep our distance hoping he doesn't see us."

"If he had training through our military or the CIA there could be a problem." Detective Fisher, "If he spotted us, I would think he would have tried to lose us by now."

"Where do you think he's heading?"

"Not a populated area Amy. My guess is that Mr. Thorn has our un-sub hiding in a wealthy area of Hammonton."

"I thought that all of Hammonton was a wealthy area?"

"Amy, as far as I know most of Hammonton is upper middle to wealthy income earners."

"He's pulling over. I wonder if Mr. Thorn spotted us"

"We are going to stay back here and see what this guy does."

"There is nothing worse then tailing someone only to blow your cover after you reach a destination your gut instincts tell you is the right place."

"I've blown a couple chances to bust people early on."

"Those are un-necessary risks that all law enforcement officers deal with at one time or another. We learn from these mistakes and move on."

"Those who haven't learned are no longer with us." Goldstein, "So now we wait and hope that Mr. Thorn leads us right to our un-sub."

"Don't forget Amy that we can't arrest this individual. I just want to learn who this un-sub is and what led them to commit these acts."

"Do you think that our un-sub is in the house?"

"I hope so, it's time to close this case and move on one way or another. We are going to wait a few minutes. I'm going to make a call to a friend of mine at the FBI." Fisher who looks quite drained of energy finds his friend at the FBI on his cell phone. "Mike, you really need a new cell phone, that phone looks like it's about to die. Come to think of it, you look like you need to take at least a couple days off."

"Look at this house Amy. I bet they have a nice big yard with a built in pool. I wouldn't be surprised if they had a large Jacuzzi."

"Are you okay Mike?"

"Yeah Amy I'm okay. Let's wait until I get a hold of my friend." Just then, Fisher's cell phone rings and it's his friend Lenny Wolf calling from the FBI. "Hello Lenny, do you remember what I told you about the case involving a young female serial killer?" Agent Wolf, "I remember Mike. I'm not in the office, but down the street from you. You and your female partner Amy Goldstein are in your Ford Escape."

"You're kidding Lenny, that's you sitting in the black GMC in front of the two-story with the row of short evergreen bushes in front with the bay windows?"

"That's the house Mike."

"Do you know this guy Thorn?"

"I know of Mr. Thorn Mike, but I don't know him personally."

"Do you think this guy Thorn could be CIA or even NSA?" Agent Wolf "Most likely he is CIA or Secret Service. He might be former Secret Service during the Reagan and Senior Bush administrations."

"We have movement in the upstairs front window, the one with the red curtains. Mike, there is at least one woman in the house."

"Unless we have a warrant we have to sit and wait for enough probable cause to go in."

"Mike, I have a warrant but want to make sure we don't blow the opportunity to at least learn who this un-sub is even if we can't prosecute. I'd like to make it clear to this un-sub that if she ever hurts an innocent person again, I will personally see that she is put on the Most Wanted list. She might even want to leave the State of New Jersey or even the country."

"What if she is a real asset to our government like you said?"

"I will be fair, but firm Mike. We'll sit tight until the sunsets."

"Let me guess, were going to wait until it gets dark out?"

"By waiting, there is the possibility that Mr. Thorn might become confident enough to let our un-sub go outside for fresh air or even a swim in the pool if there is one."

"Maybe I can walk up to the gate and see if anything is going on?"

"Let's wait Amy, if we make any moves now Thorn could see us and hide the un-sub."

Fisher and Goldstein are making plans for the weekend when Fisher's cell phone rings."

"What are we doing Lenny?"

"Were going shortly, I'm waiting for a couple of patrol units from the local police, then we move in."

"I gather we still can't arrest this un-sub Lenny."

"This is true Mike. I have to follow orders. There are big people in D.C. that said no cuffs for this un-sub. They have plans for her."

"Lenny told me that we are waiting for local cops."

"Were you looking at that window Mike?"

"No I wasn't Amy, why are you asking?"

"I just saw the shadow of a petite woman and she had long straight hair."

"I'm calling Lenny." Agent Wolf answers the phone, "Lenny, Amy saw the shadow of a woman that fits the description of the un-sub. Since the chief of police can only send a few cops, I'm waiting for a couple of agents I know. This isn't a television show like Criminal Minds or CSI NY where SWAT shows up on the scene and breaks down the door."

"What did Agent Wolf have to say?"

"We have to wait until two other agents and local police show up."

"By then, this guy Thorn could take off with the un-sub out the back of the house."

"Amy, I feel the same way you do, but when the FBI is involved there are procedures they want to follow."

"You don't want to upset your friend thinking he won't help you with any cases in the future."

"Amy, aside from being crazy about you; remember, you and I were made partners because the chief and captain want you to work with a veteran detective. You are a good detective, but if you want to be a great detective, you need to be more patient."

The sun has set and it's a clear night when two black and white Dodge Chargers pull up down the street facing Detectives Fisher and Goldstein, parked opposite side of the street from Special Agent Wolf. Shortly after the police park their cars, a man pulls up in a gray GMC Envoy. The man who gets out of the Envoy is Robert Franks, a CIA Operative. "It's him."

"Who is he Mike?" Fisher, "I know Robert from my time in the Marines. I based my decisions on instincts when handling cases as a military police official while he believes using technology is more effective in solving cases then traditional techniques. Agent Wolf, Sinclair, and CIA operative Franks all meet. Franks "Hi Mike, it's been a long time. We all want the same thing Mike; we want to meet this young lady."

"My partner and I have been working on this case for weeks and now you show up with Lenny and his brother in-law. What do you hope to gain by being involved in this case Robert?" Frank's, "I'd like to see this young lady work for the NSA not the CIA."

"You work for the CIA, why do you want this woman to work for the NSA?" Frank's, "Because our country needs this woman working in our country not overseas." Detective Goldstein "Why don't we stop wasting our time out here and find a way into that house before Thorn sees us out here and all the work we have done means nothing." Detective Fisher, "My partner is right, its time for us to move on this one." Agents Wolf and Sinclair also agree and the three officers are Lt. John Kelly, who's been with the Hammonton Police for ten years, Scott Bender, (comedian cop) and Tom Brant. Agent Wolf, "Let's remember, we can't actually arrest this un-sub, the reason why we are all here is to send a message, "Not in our backyard." Goldstein, "Are we going in sir?" Agent Wolf, "Yes Detective, were going to surround the house. Lt. Kelly, I'd like for you and the two officers to go around back but take precautions in case there is a dog. We don't want to be trigger-happy either." Sinclair, "We are not dealing with that kind of criminal element if at all." The FBI agents move towards the front of the split-level house with Detectives Fisher and Goldstein, while the three officers walk around the back of the house checking for a dog before opening the gate. After opening the gate to the backyard, the cops notice smoke coming from an outdoor grill. The officers remain as quiet as possible hoping the back door will open. Meanwhile the two FBI agents and CIA operative Frank's have managed to secure the side door with a cement block so no one can exit without attracting attention, and have picked the lock to the front door and step into the house. On their right is a room with wall-to-wall carpet and upscale furniture that one must realize has been professionally decorated. The agents and both detectives hear voices coming from an area ahead of them. The agents and both the detectives split up. Agents Sinclair, Wolf, and Franks walk straight ahead while Detectives Fisher and Goldstein walk through what is probably a living room and dining room. The voices are louder as they get closer to a closed door. In the dining room a long dark mahogany stained table with eight chairs and two lamps mounted to the ceiling that were handmade along with two mahogany bureaus that hold kitchen or dining room items like a table cloth, candles, or silverware.

As soon as the two detectives hear the FBI agents announce themselves, Fisher and Goldstein lightly push through the dining room door into the kitchen. This tactic used by the two detectives is very effective for them. The three agents move in and then the detectives, but not with force. After entering the kitchen the law enforcement officers find Mr. Thorn, with a thirty five year old man named Joseph Stern, his lady friend Sarah French, both who work for federal agencies responsible for national security. Sitting with them is a petite young lady in her twenties. Mr. Thorn, "Well look who is here Detectives Fisher and Goldstein. We could name a television show after you."

"Don't try to get on my good side Mr. Thorn, why don't you formally introduce us to your newly hired killer." Mr. Thorn, "Sorry to be so rude, this is Tanya, and she isn't the killer you think she is Detective Fisher. I see you brought your friends from the FBI and three of our community's finest police officers standing guard right out back. Nice touch detectives. I haven't heard a word out of the newly famous Detective Amy Goldstein. Is that because secretly you would have grabbed at the same opportunity that was offered to Tanya?"

"Not at all Mr. Thorn, I think you are a disgusting slime ball. I think you are only capitalizing on a terrible thing that was done to her." Mr. Thorn, "You don't think Tanya knows this Detective. Our country has been capitalizing on the tragedy of others long before you, or maybe even before I was born Detective Goldstein with a smile on his face. I bet the Gentlemen with the FBI agree but won't admit it." Agent Wolf, "I'm with Detective Goldstein Mr. Thorn, I think you are a slime ball. I hope this young lady Tanya realizes this. You are going to use Tanya to go on dangerous missions in return for protecting her from any form of prosecution. Tanya, if you want to I can speak with the U.S. Attorney General's office if your actions were to protect yourself. Please consider my offer Tanya but do not take the law into your own hands again." Mr. Thorn, "Who do you think you are Agent Wolf?"

"I'm in the position to have you indicted for obstruction of justice." Mr. Thorn, "I'm on the same side as your superiors Agent Wolf. I suggest you call the director. This young lady can speak Russian, Arabic, and Hebrew Detective Fisher. Our country needs Tanya "Now more then ever," just like the saying used when President Nixon was running for re-election, real original Mr. Thorn."

"Tanya, you have a choice and we can help you." You should leave the state and not look back. Tanya, "Thank you Detective Goldstein but I really want to help our country. My parents brought me here from Israel and I want to give something back to our country." Mr. Thorn, "We aren't going to put Tanya's life at risk. We need her because she can expertly translate documents from Russian, Arabic, and Hebrew in the shortest amount of time." Goldstein, "Tanya, How did you become fluent in these languages?"

"I learned how to speak and read these languages growing up. My parents, my aunts and uncles all taught me."

"Why did you go after those young men?"

"What makes you think it was me?"

"Tanya, if we took a sample of your hair we would learn that it was you who took the lives of two people," Fisher replies. Goldstein, "Did these guys rape you?" Tanya, "If it was me, being subjected to such an incident that might cause me to lose it."

"Tanya, as you heard earlier from Mr. Thorn, I'm Special Agent Wolf from the FBI, and I'm going to say this, "Tanya," as you were told earlier don't ever do anything like this again or the next time you will be prosecuted and no one will be able to stop it," as for you Mr. Thorn, you and I will meet again. I know your motives aren't in the best interests of this young lady. I have you in my sight. Thorn, "I'm sure we are going to meet again Agent Wolf since I'm meeting with the director of the Bureau in the next few days and the Bureau will be working with the "Company" to assure success. Tanya will be playing a role in our war on terrorism, so we will meet again soon." Agent Wolf, "Until then Mr. Thorn, I'm still going to be watching you." Thorn, "I'll be watching out for you Agent Wolf." The Agents and police leave the house. Goldstein, "What now, we let this scum-bag walk?" Agent Wolf, "I hope you are talking about Thorn and not that young woman who was really abused. Yes Amy, for now he walks. Thorn and I will meet again with the support of my director. You and Mike should be proud of yourselves, you did good police work. Have you two ever considered a career with the Bureau?"

NEXT

THE DARK GENIUS

Just Scroll Down
THE DARK GENIUS
A Fisher And Goldstein Novel
Common Law Copyright 2012
This story is for mature audiences.

INTRODUCTION

This is the second story of the Fisher and Goldstein series. Three detectives of the violent crime unit find themselves investigating homicides possibly committed by serial killers. All the characters in this story are truly fictional.

The relationship between Detectives Goldstein and Fisher heats up and, Detective Amy Goldstein is faced with a dilemma she never thought could happen. She discovers a terrible truth that no amount of training could prepare her for.

CHAPTER 1

It is a snowy day on December 14, 2012. Detectives Mike Fisher and Amy Goldstein were in her cozy living room enjoying the fireplace and some down time. Looking out the window, Fisher could see the storm clouds were not relenting a bit. The two had been spending a good deal of time together; the relationship was becoming far more than purely professional. "Hey Amy" he said. "Maybe we should head out and pick up some food, just in case the weather forecasters are actually right for a change, and we do get two plus feet of snow?" Joining him at the window she said "Hmmmm. You may be right. I think we better hurry. We'll take my truck; I have four-wheel drive." He put his arm around her and pulled her close. "Not that I'd mind being snowed in with you for a few days" he said as he kissed her.

Donning their warm winter coats, the two detectives got into Detective Fisher's green Ford Escape and drove out to the market. As they got out of the truck, Detective Goldstein looked around the parking lot. "What's wrong?" he asked. "I feel like someone is watching us." At his questioning look she said, "Don't ask me why, I just have a strange feeling." Mike looked around too, but not seeing anything he said "Amy, maybe you just need to chill out a little. Maybe a glass of wine or a nice brandy will help you. We can pick it up on the way back. After all, we just closed one of the strangest cases we ever worked. It's bound to have some affect on you. Let's do some shopping, and go back to your place and relax. Lord knows, we've earned a little alone time."

"I have wine at home. You're probably right. I'm still really on edge over that whole Paraffin Glove thing" she said. Let's just get what we need and go back to my place. Are you sure you don't want to swing by and check on your place while we're out?"

"I can check on my place via the web cam, since I had cameras installed. It doesn't hurt to have the neighbors watching as well. About the biggest thing I have to worry about is my next-door neighbor using my grill when I'm not there. At least he fills the tank if he uses it."

"You actually have a neighbor who uses your gas grill when you're not home?" said Amy. "Yes. He's pretty harmless. He reminds me of Tim Taylor from the show Home Improvement. Some of the crazy things that he does and the crazy injuries that he's suffered; I sometimes laugh so hard I'm in tears. His wife is the perfect match for him. She keeps him in line. The next week should be interesting. We're getting closer to Christmas, and Tim is going to start decorating their house. He and Sharon have two boys and one girl. The boys usually help Tim set up the decorations on the ground, but Tim does the roof on his own. I should do them a favor and have an ambulance waiting, he said with a laugh. He's on a first name basis with every crew anyway. Sharon starts the Christmas tree by stringing all the color lights and then every night until a few days before Christmas, they finish and place a small angel at the top of the tree. There's at least one ambulance call every season. Tim is such a klutz he said as he shook his head."

"You were telling me some weeks ago that you decorate for Christmas too. How much decorating do you do Mike? I thought you were Jewish" said Amy. "I am, he said. I still like to decorate. Besides, they're winter decorations, so it's non-denominational. By the time I finally get them down, the spring thaw will probably be here" he said with a laugh. "I decorate the bushes near the front bay windows. I decorate the evergreen tree in the middle of my front lawn, and set up a tree in the living room, so that people can see the lights through the curtains."

"For a guy who is suppose to be Jewish, you're not acting very Jewish, Mike."

"Amy, I'm the least Jewish one in my family."

The two detectives went into the supermarket. They made it as far as the meat aisle before Amy turned to Mike again. "Are you okay Amy?" he asked. "Yes, but I still have a feeling we are being watched."

"Hey, are you going all paranoid on me or what?" He asked her. "This isn't like you." Shaking her head, they proceeded with their shopping. After picking out a couple of chickens and steaks, they walked over to the produce aisle. "Crap," said Amy. "We forgot to get coffee."

"Don't forget the creamer and milk" said Mike. "We still need dessert. I'd like to get a blueberry pie and some yogurt. And of course, don't forget whipped cream" Mike said with a big grin. "I know things we could use whipped cream for." Amy slapped him good-naturedly. "Pervert" she said.

"You know it, honey," he said. "You get us a nice desert I'll grab the creamer and milk. Meet you up front."

"I'd rather grab you," she whispered in his ear. With a wink, she was off. For a woman who had started off saying she didn't want to make love outside of marriage, she had come a long way. Mike was a good guy, he understood. But, she had changed her mind and the two were intimate but also discreet. Mike knew he was falling for her hard. But, did she feel the same way about him? Was it love or would it be friendship with benefits?

CHAPTER 2

The two detectives finished their shopping and walked over to the cashier and paid for their groceries. Detective Goldstein still couldn't shake the feeling that someone had been following her and Fisher. "Stop it" she told herself. "You're just being paranoid." Forcing her nerves aside, she and Mike drove home. After putting the groceries away, she and Mike made dinner, kissed and went to bed. She retired to her own room; she loved being with Mike, but his snoring kept her awake at times.

Amy got out of bed. Looking out of her bedroom window at the street, she spotted a car parked about half a block away. It was snowing pretty hard, and the car was fairly clean; it hadn't been there long. Now, she was even more certain that someone has been following her and Fisher. Could this person be after her? Detective Goldstein walked downstairs and put on her dark wool coat. Grabbing her binoculars, camera and service revolver, she went outside. Leaving the lights off, she went out the back door, and to the side of her house. The rows of evergreens would hide her. Goldstein tried to keep low. Hopefully she would be able to shoot a photo of the car. Then, she might be able to find out to whom the car belonged and hopefully, get some answers. Who were these people, and why were they following her? Goldstein turned on her camera and moved her hand slowly up between two lush, green bushes, parting them just enough to see through. Adjusting the zoom lens, she shot three photos and then slid over to her right just a couple of inches and shot several more. She peered through the bushes to see if the car was still there. Just then, the driver started their car. Amy decided to stay put so as not to give away her location. She stayed low and worked her way towards the back door of her house moving slowly. Goldstein heard the car and watched the headlights while the car drove past her home. It was too dark for her to see the driver. She made her way back inside the house through the kitchen door. Thinking that Mike was still asleep upstairs she walked over to her computer in the living room. She removed the memory card from her camera and put it into her laptop. The photos appeared and Goldstein is able to view the photos of the car and an image of an individual in the car.

Half to herself she wonders out loud just what kind of car is this when Fisher tells her, "It's a Subaru Outback," and Goldstein replies, "You nearly scared the crap out of me," then Fisher responds, "That could be pretty disgusting."

"Are you trying to be funny, Mike?"

"What were you doing, Amy?"

"I woke up with the feeling that someone has been watching us or just me. I went outside to check"

"Without waking me first. What the hell, Amy? Did you learn anything?"

"I'm not sure yet Mike. I just loaded these photos I took through the bushes outside before the person drove off."

"Can I try something, Amy?

I want to see if I can enlarge the photos, and see if we get a clear view of the license plate number. I'm going to download some software. It might take a little time, but we can get you some answers."

"Screw that Mike, I want to see if I got an image of this person or maybe I got a good enough photo to ID them."

"Amy" he said calmly, "Just let me go through these photos and enlarge them right on the computer."

"What do you think I should do, just sit here and watch?"

"I'll tell you what Amy, you go through the photos and I'll go make some coffee."

"That's alright Mike, you see what you can do with the photos. I'll make the coffee. You're better at working with the photography software then I am. And, I definitely make better coffee." Detective Goldstein walked into the kitchen and turned on the lights. Something was out of place. Looking around she noticed something strange. Her coffee maker has been moved. "Mike, by any chance, did you move the coffee maker before we went to bed last night?"

"No Amy, I didn't even touch the coffee maker."

"Someone's been in this kitchen Mike."

"Maybe you moved it Amy and forgot."

"No Mike, I wouldn't put the coffee maker in front of the can opener. That makes no sense. Besides, it goes on the other side of the counter. I don't move things without putting them back. You know how anal I am about things like that."

"Check the back door jam and see if there are any marks If not, there maybe at the front door. Unless someone else has the keys to your house, they would have left marks around the lock or door jam. I think you're right Amy, I think someone has been watching us or just you. We should interview some of your neighbors to find out if they saw someone sitting in a dark colored Subaru Outback."

"It's still too early to knock on the doors of my neighbors."

"Hey Amy, look at this. I just enlarged a photo and it looks like a woman was in that dark color Subaru. Unfortunately you didn't get a clear enough photo of their face or, did you get a photo of their license plate. I can only tell from the image that she is young and a brunette. I'm going to work on it some more though."

"I would like to talk to some of my neighbors today."

"Amy, I think we need to call the captain and bring him in on this as soon as possible. If we try to deal with this ourselves, both Lou and the Chief of police will be all over our butts. We don't want that in our files."

"Actually, Mike, I don't mind someone all over my ass – as long as it's you" she said, trying to lighten the mood. "Now, who's the pervert?" he said as he took her into his arms. "I didn't mean it to sound that way." Moving to the couch, they kiss. They were both excited by the case and the adrenaline rush. Passion overruled emotions and logic. They were so distracted, that they forgot about the case. So, they also forgot about the enhanced photos now uploading across the computer screen. The image of a face, a woman's face was watching them.

Finally, Mike said, "Now that we've had our little diversion, I think we need to get back to work." Getting up from the couch, Amy's eyes went to the screen. "Uh, Mike" she said, "I think we have a face to work with."

"It looks like we have an un-sub and a new case. Damn. I was hoping for a little peace and quiet. Oh, well. I'll call it in. We can work from home"

"I'm with you Mike. That's a great idea. I have a feeling that we're working a new case and it's going to be a big one."

"I think this case is going to be one of a personal nature. We are going to have to be more observant of our surroundings Amy. This un-sub is after one of us."

"This is the second female un-sub case in just a few months" said Amy. "I wondered about that myself. Can you think of someone you ticked off lately? I mean more than your regulars?"

"Why would you ask Mike?"

"Well, it might help us to get an idea of who was sitting in the car last night watching the house. You did say that you had a strong feeling that someone was watching you or us yesterday. We might be dealing with someone who may indeed come after us and I would like to have an idea who the person might be. Maybe it's a classmate that one of us ticked off?"

"Mike, you said that the car she was sitting in was a Subaru Outback?"

"That's right Amy."

"Could you tell from the photos of the Subaru if it is a newer model?"

In the back of Detective Goldstein's mind was one big question. Could it be someone she knows? Someone she was once friendly with and now this person is after her? Detective Goldstein was trying to think of someone she might have ticked off while growing up. Detective Fisher is thinking to himself that their un-sub is after his partner. A partner he is in love with and would like to marry someday. While Goldstein is in the kitchen making coffee, Mike keeps asking himself, who is after Amyl? He looks at his watch. It's 7:00 AM in the morning and is it too early to call Lou Costello, their Captain. Fisher remembers when he called Costello early one time and he told Fisher that the next time he calls him that early again it had better be for a very big case. With a resigned sigh, he dialed the number. As usual, there was no cell service. Damn cell phone service. He went back into the den to try the landline. Fisher was thinking to himself "What's bigger then someone that might be after a detective or any law enforcement officer."

Detective Goldstein is in the kitchen making them coffee when she gets a feeling that someone is right outside her kitchen. She looked up and there is a female face looking right at her, through one of her icy kitchen windows. Dropping the coffee cups on the counter, she fumbled for her gun. Hearing the crash of the falling cups, Fisher jumped up from the chair and asked, "What's going on Amy?" The next thing Fisher hears is Amy saying, "I can't believe you just did that, Ellen. You just scared the living crap out of me. Didn't anyone ever tell you sneaking up on a cop can be a really bad idea? I could have shot you."

"Whose truck is outside your house?" Asked Ellen "Mike, this is my sister Ellen."

"Hi Ellen, pleased to finally have the opportunity to meet you. Are all the women in your family as pretty as you ladies are?"

"You really had to ask that question, Mike? "He's just charming Amy, isn't he?"

"That's just the way Mike is Ellen. What are you doing here?"

"Someone was in Dad's house when no one was home the other day."

"How do you know that Ellen, did they leave a mess or burglarize the house?"

"No Amy, I found my clothes on the floor and all over my bedroom."

"Amy, I'm missing a couple outfits. They're really pretty and really expensive. I know they were there."

"Are you serious? Have you checked the washer or dryer, have you been to mom's house and maybe left them there?"

"I've checked everywhere Amy. I haven't been at mom's house that much lately. I'm staying at my friend Jennifer's place for a week or so while my place is being painted."

"Does dad know what happened?"

"Dad knows, Amy that's all I'm going to say. You know how he looks at things." I haven't told Mom; she'll just get all freaked out."

"Right away, he's blaming you."

"And then he says that we like to flirt with guys and this is why we have had problems with guys. That's such a bunch of crap, Ellen, and you know it. I'd let you stay here but I've got a problem of my own and I can't discuss it with you. I think it best you stay with your friend Jennifer rather then stay here."

"From the look on your face Amy, you must be dealing with someone who could be very dangerous. What does your partner think?"

"Mike's concerned"

"You got photos of this person last night?"

"They didn't come out well, but he's trying to enhance them some."

"That's a shame Amy. You and Mike seem to get some really strange cases."

"Ellen, this is only the fourth case Mike and I have worked together."

"What about the case with the students at Stockton Village Condos who were being raped?"

"I didn't work that case with Mike. Those residents were taken advantage of while they were intoxicated. They knew the guys who took advantage of them and refused to file any charges, claiming it was their own fault as many victims of assault believe."

"Dad said they were asking for it because of the way they dressed or flirted with guys in the community."

" Ellen, you have to remember that our father was raised in a strict environment. After he left home, he met and married mom. He certainly can not go back, just as if he were Amish."

Mike had already walked back into the living room and was sitting back at the desk studying the photos. Mike's face turned pale white as one of the photos he's been working on clears up some. He stares at the photo, not yet saying anything to his partner or her sister. When Amy asks her partner if he has found anything yet, he replies "No such luck yet."

Deep down inside Detective Fisher is becoming concerned of who their un-sub might be. To Detective Fisher an image in his mind is beginning to disturb him. Fisher decides to put his coat on and go outside to make a call to Captain Costello and ask for a background check.

"Ladies I'm going outside to my truck and I also have to make a call. For some reason, I'm not getting a good connection in the house this morning."

"What's up with him?"

"Mike has that wireless service I don't have to mention the name."

While sitting in his truck Mike finally gets a hold of his captain. "Good morning Captain. Sorry to call you so early in the morning."

"Don't worry Mike, you got lucky. I was already up brewing some coffee. I had to go back to the old fashioned coffee pot on the kitchen stove. My kids are the only ones who can get the coffee maker to work. That coffee maker drives me crazy."

"Why drive? It's a short walk."

"Ha! Mike, that was really funny."

"You actually heard me whisper that time?"

"Damn wireless service" he thought. His wireless service works better when he doesn't want it to. "Yes, Mike. Now what's going on?"

"I'd like to ask for a background check on Ellen Goldstein. I'd like to know what kind of car she might own, or if she rented a Subaru Outback? I think we have a problem Captain. I think that Amy's younger sister might be up to no good."

"Why do you feel that her sister is up to no good?"

"Yesterday at the supermarket, Amy felt that she or the both of us were being watched. Then, last night or early this morning Amy went outside while I was still asleep and took photos of someone in a dark color Subaru Outback. After studying the photos Amy had taken, I discovered an image of a young woman in the photos. I almost wonder if the image is Amy's sister"

"Are you saying Mike that Amy's sister Ellen is after her own sister? I've heard of sibling rivalry but one sister going after another sister to hurt them is really over the top Mike."

"So you think we are looking at another un-sub?" The Captain asked. "I didn't even know that there was a problem involving Amy until you just told me what has been going on Mike. Just keep an eye on Amy Mike. Maybe I should have her take sometime off? The case of the Paraffin Glove was a little on the strange side. Now, from what you are telling me is that Amy believes that she is being watched when the woman in the car might have been looking to see if a husband or boyfriend is cheating on them." The Captain said. "Captain, do you think Amy is becoming paranoid?"

"I'm no expert on mental health issues Mike, and there isn't anything in Amy's file with the department to indicate any issues. Amy might be right. There might be someone after her or both of you."

"Yeah, Captain, Amy and I may have ticked off some big shots."

"Don't forget Mr. Thorn from the CIA while you were both handling the case of The Paraffin Glove. He was definitely not pleased with either one of us"

"Come to think of it Captain, Amy and I have handled some strange cases since she joined our team. Now it seems like we have another one. Amy and I are becoming more like Molder and Scully in the X-Files."

"Jackson just walked in my house probably wanting a cup of coffee before we leave for the department so hold on a minute. Leon, the cups we are taking with us are over there with the lids, you can pour me one and then you can call and ask Steve Schultz to do a background check on Ellen Goldstein. I want to know what kind of car this young lady might be driving?"

CHAPTER 3

•

"Is your computer working, boss?"

"Yes it is Leon."

"Good, I'm going to use it to do the background check myself and have the answers by the time we get to the department."

"Are you still on the phone, Mike?"

"Yes I am, Captain."

"Jackson's on my computer trying to do a background check when I can't even use my computer to send out checks through my online banking account. Jackson's good with computers. Me, I like digging through stacks of boxes for my answers. Or. Just good old-fashioned police work. Ask questions, the investigation and arrest, all of it. Mike, sometimes I feel like its time for me to retire. I just can't keep up with the new gadgets or video screens that allow us to make photos larger, right on the screen, I feel like we are doing a television episode of NCIS."

"Captain, think of all the cases we solved prior to having all this technology. In the end, Captain, it's still the traditional police work that enabled us to solve and close cases. Think how many families have closure thanks to our hard work without the use of technology."

"I've got to get back inside boss. I'm freezing my stones off out here."

It's not just Detective Fisher who is concerned about his partner and a woman he is falling totally in love with, it's their captain who wants Fisher to keep a close eye on Amy, and keep in touch with his boss. Meanwhile, Detective Jackson has been unable to learn who owns the Subaru. What Jackson did learn is that Subaru only manufactures a certain amount of

Outback models in black or dark blue for each region of the U.S. Market unless however, customers ordered these Subaru's special and no residents in the entire State of New Jersey had recently specially ordered a new Outback. But this had not been any stock Subaru Outback. The pictures showed custom rims and a gray color grill. This one should be easy to spot. Loaded with after-market parts, this was one tricked out ride.

Leon Jackson, "You know Mike I never cared for the term "African American." I just think of myself as a Black man who was fortunate to have a great mother even if she was at work ten hours a day. Not that this has anything to do with the case we are all working on but it was my mother who taught me self-discipline and patience and I consider myself to be the most fortunate one of all the kids on the street where I grew up. My mother taught me the values of hard work and honesty and here I am today."

"Your right Leon, I didn't know that your father was killed while serving our country and it was your mother who raised you on her own. You're a good detective and a decent person. I enjoy working with you."

"Thanks Mike, I enjoy working with you as well."

"I learn from working with you too, Leon. You have computer knowledge and I would like you to teach me how to obtain information on the Internet and inter— agency information when working on a case."

"That's just fine Mike. I'll teach you a little bit a couple times a week and watch as you use the computer to obtain information on suspects or as we say un-subs. Is that okay with you?"

"Thanks Leon."

"I learned that there were only a few Subaru Outback's with the same colors sold in this area. Captain, now that I obtained this information, we have to go to the department because we can't get into the DMV data base to learn who owns these Subaru's on this computer."

"Why can't you go on the data base from this computer?"

"Captain, it would be illegal even though both of us are cops. As police officials, we are not to have any connections setup in our homes to use the DMV database or many other government agency computers. Where's the family at Captain?"

"Karen is visiting her sister and my kids are grown so they do whatever they choose. For the most part they are working."

"Glad to hear the family is doing well, Captain. To me, family is everything."

"Look outside Leon, the snow is really coming down."

"Good, I love when it snows around Christmas and it would be even better if it would snow on Christmas evening."

"You're a hopeless romantic Leon."

"So are you Captain. You wouldn't have all those lights setup with the Santa and Reindeer on the roof of your house if you weren't a hopeless romantic. "Well, we had better take my truck, your car is rear wheel drive and not so good in this weather."

"Thanks Jackson, although Karen and I do own a 2008 Jeep Liberty, she took it."

The Captain and Detective Jackson had finished their coffee, put the mugs in the dishwasher then they fill a couple of cups to go, then they put their coats and hats on, the captain sets the alarm system for his home, and they walk out the front door. Jackson started up his Ford pickup truck while the captain uses one of the brushes to clean off the right side and half of the back window, Detective Jackson cleans off the windows on the driver's side and rear window. Captain Costello and his family live in a two-story house with a sub basement. They also have two separate garages but one of them is not seen from the street and was turned into a combination workshop, storage area, and even a place for someone to live in above the shop area. The two Leo's (Law Enforcement Officers) are on their way to the department.

"Do you know what it's going to be like later Captain if the snow keeps coming down this heavy through the day?"

"It's going to be heavy snow and this means a bad one Leon." Jackson, "I love it. This is just one of the reasons why I got this Ford. This truck gets better gas mileage then the older ones, even when it's in four wheel drive. I can even shift right into four-wheel drive as long as I'm going slow. You know you can't do that with a Jeep, boss. You can do some damage or at least you will probably need to get the Jeep serviced at least on the older Jeeps."

"Our Liberty is a 2008, not one of the older ones."

"Boss, if you check the manual it probably tells you not to put your jeep in four- wheel drive unless you are stopped at the time. I get the 4X4 magazine, and all the articles have said, that although the Jeep is the original when it comes to 4X4 driving and what needs to be done in order to get many years of fun and dependability, aside from regular service and the right tires, one article after another stated that Jeeps are great 4X4's but to be in a stopped position before engaging the unit. I'll give you one of the magazines I kept."

Shortly after arriving at the police department, Detective Jackson goes in the room where he can use one of the computers to go on the DMV database and try to learn the identities of the twenty-five people who own Subaru Outback's in Atlantic County. If he accomplishes this, then he can limit the search. While trying to limit his search for names of people who own Subaru Outback's in the area, Jackson finds no one who is related to Detective Goldstein unless the car is under another name or it was purchased used. Detective Jackson was once profiled by the FBI as an obsessive- compulsive personality. Once he gets his mind on something he doesn't stop until he either gets what he wants or learns that his efforts are a waste of time. When the DMV site starts to freeze up, Jackson asks Officer DePaul sitting on his right if the officer can bring up the phone number for the main office of the DMV in Trenton. In just thirty seconds Jackson is given the phone number and calls the DMV in Trenton with a request. Does anyone with the name of Ellen Goldstein own a Subaru Outback, and if so, what year, what color, and where does she live?

At the main office is Sarah Merkel who tells Detective Jackson, "It's going to take at least a couple of hours to check the database for anyone with her name or anyone connected to her."

CHAPTER 4

"The car may not even be in her name. It might belong to another relative or a friend."

"Do whatever you can Ms. Merkel, and thank you for your assistance." Detective Jackson turns to Officer DePaul and says "Thank you John for your help."

"Any time Leon. You helped me with my first report and the bosses couldn't believe that not only was everything concise, but they were even more impressed when I told them that you assisted me a lot in completing my first arrest report."

"Honesty does pay in the long run my friend."

"It sure does. What's going on Leon? Anything I might be able to do to help?"

"If you see a young lady in her late teens or early twenties driving a dark color Subaru Outback, don't make her feel as though she's under suspicion for anything, just ask her for her driver's license number, owner's registration, and auto insurance card. Make sure you write down her driver's license number and policy number for her insurance, make a note of when you write everything down and unless she does anything wrong like blowing a red light, let her go."

"Wait a minute Leon, I was doing a residential drive through last night and I saw a young lady, really cute, a brunette, really attractive, first at a WAWA and then I'm sure the same lady sitting on a street with her lights off in her car, it wasn't running, and she was sipping the cup of coffee I saw her purchase at WAWA only a few miles from here. I had Fred Warner do a drive by as well, to see if she was still there an hour later."

"Was the lady still sitting there in the Subaru?"

"According to Fred she was still there. A matter of fact if you ask Fred he found it kind of strange that this young lady was sitting in her car for so long with no blanket or heat on in her car when it was really cold out."

"Thank you John."

Detective Jackson walked over to Captain Costello's office to inform him. "Captain, I was just talking to Officer DePaul who said that both he and Officer Fred Warner not only saw the young lady on the street near Goldstein's home sipping coffee she bought at a nearby WAWA, they found it interesting that the woman's car wasn't running so she could stay warm. Officer Warner saw the woman an hour later sitting at the same location."

"Now we are making some progress."

"I hope I didn't overstep your authority Captain, since I asked Officer DePaul if he an officer Warner see this young lady again, just to ask for her driver's license, registration and insurance card and make a note of the information, and unless she blows a traffic light let her go."

"That's fine Leon, but the next time, please ask me first. Okay?"

"I understand Captain." Detective Jackson started to walk out of his Captain's office when Captain Costello says "Good idea Leon. I'm putting a good note in your file."

"Is Mike staying close to Amy?"

"Yes, I want him to keep an eye on Amy. Her sister showed up at the house earlier this morning." Shortly after leaving Captain Costello's office, Detective Jackson learns from Officer John DePaul that the Town Council for Egg Harbor chose a new Chief of Police.

"Captain, I Just heard that a new Chief of Police was chosen."

"Did they choose Michael Stone?"

"How did you know that Captain?"

"He's a good man. I use to work with Michael while in the Navy, then I came here and he went to work for the FBI and in the BAU."

"Where did I hear of the BAU before?"

"Come on Leon, the BAU is the Behavioral Analysis Unit. Where's your head? You know that. What's wrong with you?"

"This might be the best time for him to become the chief."

"Are you talking about this case Leon?"

"Yes Captain. I wonder why someone is after Amy, and if this new chief is an expert on profiling, isn't that what we need right now?"

"This is going to be a strange case. Where is Officer DePaul? "I'll get him, he just went to get himself a cup of coffee."

"I want to see him in my office in five minutes." A few minutes later Officer John DePaul walks into the Captain's office. "Officer DePaul, I want you and Officer Warner to patrol Detective Goldstein's neighborhood more often." Captain Costello picks up the phone in his office and calls Detective Fisher. "Mike, I don't want Amy interviewing any of her neighbors, okay. I don't want you and Amy talking about this matter with her sister. We have a new Chief of Police and he is a former FBI Profiler. Keep that to yourself for now."

"Are you okay with this new chief Captain?"

"I'm fine Mike. I'm worried about Amy. Something isn't right here."

"I agree with you Captain, something is up."

"What's going on Mike?"

"I'll tell you later, Amy. Why don't we make some breakfast Amy? Do you eat breakfast Ellen?"

"Yes I do Mike and thank you for offering."

"Good, I'll cook up some eggs. Amy, do you want toast?"

"I'll get the bread and butter." I'll get the dishes and silverware out."

"Thanks, Ellen. Can you put the napkins out too?"

Not realizing it, Detective Fisher is intently watching Ellen as she places the silverware and napkins on the table. Fisher is really waiting for the opportunity to take something that Ellen has handled so that he can put it aside hoping to get at least one finger and hand print, whether it is a napkin, coffee cup, fork, knife, or spoon. Fisher notices a syringe lying in Ellen's pocket book and wonders why.

CHAPTER 5

He is trying not to draw attention to himself. Detective Fisher doesn't want Amy to know what he is trying to do. Fisher believes that Ellen might be up to something and has some concerns for the way Amy has been acting over the past twenty-four hours. Maybe the two sisters have been keeping a secret about their past? Maybe Ellen knows something about Amy and is using it against her own sister? Fisher cooks the eggs and hash browns while Amy gets the bread ready for toasting and Ellen after setting the table opens the refrigerator to find a couple cartons of orange juice, milk, and half and half creamer.

"Hey Amy, I didn't know you were such a big fan of orange juice?"

"Actually Ellen, I had one carton of juice, it was Mike who bought the second one."

"Should I take one of the cartons out for breakfast?"

"Sure Ellen? I drink a glass of orange juice at least a few times a week, do you?"

"I like orange juice once or twice a week." Detective Fisher would love to get one of Ellen's fingerprints from the carton but knows that he could attract too much attention and if Ellen hasn't done anything wrong, he doesn't want to hurt her feelings.

Something else is starting to concern Detective Fisher. Fisher excuses himself telling Amy and her sister that he needs to run outside and make a call to his folks. Fisher calls Captain Costello. "Captain can, you or Leon do background checks on the medical histories of Amy, her sister and parents?"

"What are you looking for Mike?"

"I'm not sure yet Captain. But shake a tree and see what falls from it."

"Okay Mike, Leon and I will checkout the family history and let you know. I gather were not just talking basic medical histories but more?"

"Yes Captain, I'm looking for more information."

"You don't quite know yet, do you Mike?"

"No I don't Captain." Detective Fisher is beginning to wonder if he is wrong because the two sisters seem to get along great together. He just wants to make sure that his partner is going to be okay. That her sister just wants for the two of them to hangout together. Fisher decides to take the direct approach by asking Ellen why she just came over. "Although we never met before, I'm surprised you just decided to stop by and visit?"

"I haven't seen Amy in weeks. All we did was talk on the phone once a week and we usually get together and hang out. I figured that Amy must have met a guy she really loves and that's why we haven't gotten together."

"Well Ellen, it's not that Mike and I really loved each other at first, we were dealing with a strange murder case."

"Now I think we have another case." Fisher walks away from the two ladies and calls Captain Costello. "I think were wasting time looking into Amy or her family's medical history."

"Not so fast Mike. When Leon got busy helping our new chief, I decided to do some investigating on my own. Amy and her sister have dealt with some real hardship. I found the divorce between both her parents through a search on the Internet. "I don't sense any anger between the two sisters. They seem to get along together."

"There is the possibility that someone is after the two of you? Leon thinks that Amy's sister came to visit hoping to meet and see what you are like."

"Does Leon think that Amy's sister Ellen has issues with her sister being in a serious relationship?"

"No, Leon being into reading books on psychology feels that her younger sister might be upset if you too get married because she won't have as much time to spend with her older sister."

"Ask Leon, isn't the sister considering that if Amy and I have a child together that we would want Ellen in our lives even more?"

"I'll ask Leon later, he's helping our new chief. The Chief is having problems with his laptop. So you and I might not hear back from Leon until about 2:00 PM. If this snow doesn't stop I'm going to need Leon to take me home later. My wife has our Jeep."

"Leon has that truck and can't he plow out your driveway for you?"

"Yes he does Mike, and I'm going to ask him to plow the driveway for me. I have a call coming in Mike. I'll call you if it's important."

The captain ends his call with Detective Fisher to find out what the other call is about. Detective Jackson tells the captain that as Amy and her siblings got older they seem to grown stronger. Detective Jackson learned this from a search he did. Jackson believes this might be the reason why Amy seems distant and not always friendly then some other women in her age group.

"I would think we would be looking at the opposite end of the spectrum when it comes to emotional well being."

"That's been the belief by many doctors and counselors who have worked in the social services field for years. Studies are still being done on what happens to kids when the parents grow apart and the kids are still young."

"Thanks for the information Leon I'll pass it on to Mike."

"Leon, can you plow my driveway when you take me home later?"

"No problem Captain. It's good that your garage isn't located directly at the end of the driveway. I'll even help you with some wood for your stove and fireplace."

"I don't use logs for the fireplace just for the wood burning stove in the kitchen."

"What time do you think we should leave today Captain?"

"I think we should leave at 1:00 to get some lunch at the Diamond Diner I'd like to stop off at the mini mart near my home because I asked the owner if he could put some artificial logs and wood pellets for the pellet stove aside for my wife and I."

"I didn't know you had a pellet stove."

"That was installed down the hall from the bedrooms."

"Mike, Leon didn't find anything bad when doing a search on the girls or their brothers."

"That's good to hear "No problem Captain. I'm not getting any bad vibes from either one of the sisters. I think Ellen came to visit her sister because she just wanted to see Amy. As the old saying goes "Only time will tell." Fisher has noticed that the snow is coming down even harder then it was just a half hour ago. What he's curious about is how Ellen made it to her sister's house. Fisher wonders what kind of car Ellen drove to Amy's. Then he asked her. "I drove here Mike."

"What kind of car do you drive?"

"Yeah Ellen, you were going to tell me what kind of car you were buying a couple weeks ago and never called or sent me a text."

"Sorry Amy, I got really busy with a project I started; and no I'm not telling you anything about the project just yet. As for the type of car I just bought, I got a Subaru Outback wagon."

"What color is it?" It's blue with gray color panels along the bottom of the car. I got a demo Amy but it has an excellent stereo, sunroof, fog lights, and a real spare tire, not a doughnut. I got all sorts of gadgets installed including a state of the art security system."

CHAPTER 6

When Ellen tells Detective Fisher and Amy that she bought a Subaru Outback that is blue in color with gray color panels at the bottom of the car, this information really sticks with Fisher while Detective Goldstein thinks nothing of it because it's her sister's car. Fisher thinks that maybe he just needs to cool it. He needs to step back because he's too close with Amy to think clearly. Detective Fisher tells the ladies he's going outside to clean off his truck in case he and Detective Goldstein need to go out to a crime scene. His real reason for going out to his truck is to call Captain Costello for some advice.

"Captain, this is Mike, I wonder if my being too close to Amy is affecting my judgment?"

"Mike, I've been your boss for over five years and you are one of the best detectives I've ever worked with. Don't question your own judgment that can be dangerous. The best thing you can do is to not only stay close to Amy, be the best partner you have been, and the friend you have been to Amy. I know you love her and this is the reason why you are calling me. Mike, this proves to me even more why you need to stay where you are."

"Thanks Captain. I just wonder if I'm too close."

"If I thought it was bad for you to remain there I would have told you to go home and I would have sent Richard Stokes there. No Mike, you are the best one to handle this. So stay with her."

"Okay Captain."

"Leon and I are getting ready to leave for the diner to have lunch, than he's going to take me to pickup some artificial logs and pellets for the pellet stove, then drop me off at home and plow my driveway. Then I can throw some sand and Ice-melt so the driveway and sidewalk won't be so slippery."

"Is Leon going to plow the sidewalk, too?"

"I have a neighbor whose son has a plow and they do the sidewalk for Karen and I. So, you stay with Amy Mike. If you need to reach me later, call my home or cell phone. I made sure it's charged and in my coat pocket."

After getting off the phone with Detective Fisher, Captain Costello called dispatch and reminds the Sergeant, to have officers DePaul and Warner patrol the area around Detective Goldstein's home just so there will be less of an opportunity for someone to break in to Detective Goldstein's home. Captain Costello is worried that someone is after Detective Goldstein. He makes a note for himself to call Detective Fisher later on in the day and at least once at night. Costello grabs a few cigars Then Captain Costello shuts off the lights to his office and lets Detective Jackson know he's ready to leave for the diner. With the exception of smoking cigars, Captain Costello takes good care of himself. The captain eats meals that are high in fiber; he enjoys drinking a glass of red wine while he sits either on the front porch in the summer or the enclosed porch in the winter while having a cigar. Often the Captain will listen to jazz or classical music and read the newspaper if it actually shows up at the front door. If not, he will use his laptop to read the news. Captain Costello and Detective Jackson finish their meals at the Diamond Diner near the Cardiff Circle where they enjoy eating. Detective Jackson "Next time Captain, let's go to the Shore Diner on Fire Road I like their desserts. There isn't anything wrong with the meals here but I like the other diner more for their desserts." Mean while the snow is still coming down. Costello and Jackson leave for the mini mart to pickup logs and wood pellets then to the Captain's home. As soon as they arrive at the captain's home, Detective Jackson engages the plow on his truck, "Stand by Captain I'm going to plow the snow on the drive way for you."

"Here Leon take the money. Use it towards gas for the truck and don't say no."

"I have to throw some melt away on the drive way and at the side and front doors."

As the captain throws the melt away around with old coffee cans, the captain and Leon notice that the snowfall is not as heavy as it was when they first arrived. "We're done with throwing this stuff for now Leon. Let me get the door open and then you go home to your family Leon. Don't forget to call me when you get home." I'll call you when I get home Captain. "I only live a few blocks away and it will only take me two minutes to plow my driveway."

Detective Jackson plows out his driveway as soon as he arrives home. His kids and their friends must have cleared the sidewalk and they made two paths to both the front and side doors. Detective Jackson considers himself one of the most fortunate of law enforcement officials when it comes to his family and the people he works with. His wife a medical doctor, a graduate of the University of Pennsylvania Medical School, his three kids who bring home above average grades from school, and even their friends who come over and they all study together. Still, Detective Jackson is concerned about one of his fellow detectives whose life could be in danger, or maybe one of his favorite detectives is having problems that he could not understand. He backs his truck into the driveway like he usually does in the winter when there is a chance for snow he shuts off the engine, gets out of the truck and walks into his home and says hello to everyone and tells his wife Doris that he wants to let the captain know he got home safely and to make sure his boss is okay as well.

"Isn't Karen home Leon?"

"No, Doris, she went to visit her sister or one of their kids. She took their Jeep."

"You can bet the captain told her to."

"It seems like we have a full house this evening."

"Our kid's friends from next door Leon. Donna and Jim had to run over to the hospital because her sister had surgery for acid reflex and they went to pick her up since she can't stay at home alone for weeks."

"It sounds like serious surgery Doris?"

"Yes, but not as bad as the doctors originally thought. She won't be skiing for a month."

"I have something on my mind Doris in case you didn't realize."

"We have been married for fifteen years Leon so I know when something is bothering you."

"One of our Detectives has been very nervous lately. From what I was told, this detective believes someone has been watching them."

"Maybe they are tired. Has the detective been suffering from nausea?"

"Why would you ask, Doris?"

"She might be pregnant Leon."

"What's that got to do with it? I'll call anyway." Detective Jackson calls his boss and tells him what Doris told him and to ask Mike if Amy has been dealing with nausea, that she might be pregnant or dealing with a virus that's going around."

"I'll call Mike and ask him to ask Amy if she's been dealing with nausea. Thanks Leon. I'll call you later."

Detective Fisher was just walking into Amy's house after cleaning off his truck when he heard his cell phone. A quick check of the caller ID showed it was Captain Costello. "Hello Captain. Did you get home yet?"

"Yeah Mike, Leon drove me home a while ago. He just called me to ask you if Amy has been dealing with nausea." "Why do you ask?"

"For two reasons, first, she might have a virus that's going around, and second, she might be pregnant."

"I'm not sure if I want to mention the second reason if Amy is even dealing with nausea, but let me ask her. Amy, have you been dealing with nausea lately?"

"Not at all Mike." No nausea Captain."

"Has she been taking new a medication lately?"

"Amy, the captain is on the phone and wants to know if you are taking any new medications?"

"Yes I have been."

"Amy said she is taking new medication."

"Ask Amy to go on the Internet and look up the side effects to the medication. It's none of my business what she is taking unless it would interfere with her doing her job. This might be why she has been feeling as though someone is watching her."

"You mean the medication she is taking is making her feel paranoid?"

"Some medications cause some interesting side effects."

"I'm sorry Captain but I'm beginning to believe that Amy's well being is at risk but I'm not sure who is after Amy. I think it's time for us to treat this as a threat against one of our own and for me to inform Amy that we are going to put her under protective custody."

"Good luck with that one Mike."

"Amy, I just got off the phone with the captain. He feels that you should go online and check the side effects of any new medications you're taking."

"Why does the captain want me to do that, does he think I'm going nuts?" No, Mike says, "The captain thinks you might be having side effects from medication. I think someone is really after you Amy."

"How much weight do you carry in the department Mike?" Ellen asks. "Well Ellen, there have been some changes in the department so I'm not sure. I did learn that we are going to have another detective in our unit."

"We really have a new detective joining our unit Mike?"

"Yes Amy, but they haven't arrived yet. I was told they had more hand to hand combat experience and they are able to speak and understand different languages Amy. We are also going to have a new chief. Oh well, I let that slip."

"What happened to our last chief of police?"

"He will be the new Assistant Commissioner of Public Safety. Right now Amy I'm worried about you."

"Why are you worried about me Mike?"

"Because I believe someone is after you Amy. I believe your life is in serious danger. Captain Costello and Leon have been looking at all possibilities, Amy. They originally thought that you were having a break down."

"What are you going to do to protect my sister?"

"Right now, Ellen, we are going to stay here, and there will be more police patrols in this neighborhood."

"What are you going to do to prevent someone from hurting Amy?"

"Amy, I want you to keep the light on in the hallway."

"I do have outdoor lights that come on when someone is walking around the outside of the house."

"I think its best Amy if you and Ellen slept in the room with the two beds and I'll sleep in your room. This way if someone does break in tonight to come after you, they will be thrown off when they don't see you but find me instead."

While Detective Fisher is telling his partner and her sister that police patrols are being increased, he wants changes where they will sleep, Mike Fisher has some suspicion of who is behind this but not sharing anything. Detective Fisher is considering the past few cases he and Amy worked on together. He again, is considering the last case he and Amy worked involving Mr. Thorn from the CIA who kind of reminds him of the character Trent Cort in the original NCIS show. Mr. Thorn isn't above sending someone to do surveillance of his partner and girlfriend Detective Goldstein.

What Detective Fisher is wondering is if Thorn is behind this. Is he looking for a way to get even with his partner and possibly cause her harm figuring she is an easier target or is Thorn considering Detective Goldstein for a position with the CIA or was Thorn really with the NSA (National Security Agency) and Thorn didn't exactly say what agency he worked for.

Detective Fisher decides to call his friend Agent Wolf of the FBI. Agent Wolf would be able to learn if Thorn ordered surveillance of his partner. Detective Fisher takes his cell phone out of its clip and to bring up his friend Lenny's phone number and call him. "Hello Mike, how are you doing?"

"I'm fine Lenny but there is a problem regarding Detective Goldstein. She is being followed and I have concern for her safety. Would you be able to find out if Thorn is in the area or has placed my partner under surveillance for some reason?" Agent Wolf, "Let me make some phone calls for you Mike. I'll get back to you later."

"Can you make this a priority Lenny?"

"I'll make some calls Mike and try to learn if Mr. Thorn is having your partner followed or if she is under surveillance. Maybe Thorn thinks your partner being a woman would be helpful in our country's war on terrorism?"

CHAPTER 7

After ending his call with his long-time friend, Detective Fisher is again thinking that there is more to his partner being followed. Fisher knows that he and Detective Goldstein have made their share of enemies. Fisher realizes that they could be dealing with someone who has an ax to grind with Amy, maybe even someone who works for the police department and who is angry because they weren't offered the same opportunities as his partner. Detective Fisher makes a note for himself to have his captain do some checking to see if there are officers in the department that might be out to get even with his partner.

Detective Fisher notices that the snow is coming down again but not as heavy as it was earlier. He tells his partner and her sister that he is going outside to get some logs for the fireplace. Amy tells him that he only needs to get a few since she has some Dura Flame artificial logs. Fisher tells his partner, "It's not safe to use those logs with traditional wood."

"Mike, I checked with someone I know at the fire department down the street, and they said it's okay to use a Dura Flame log to start a fire in your fireplace but after twenty minutes or so, you can add a log. You don't put them in together."

"Really, I never heard that before." Amy walks over to her partner and boyfriend and asks him, "Do you think the person who has been watching me is someone I know personally or someone we investigated and arrested?"

"Actually Amy, I think it's someone closer than you think. It might be an officer in the department."

"Do you have any ideas Mike?"

"No Amy, because it just popped into my head. You moved up the ranks to detective more quickly then others in your own age group. I'm asking the captain to run a check on some of the officers you worked with. "I don't feel its another officer, I think it's personal."

"Give me some idea of who you think it might be and I will run a check on them. I think it might be a family member."

"I don't think it's a family member but don't know exactly who might be after me Mike."

"Maybe it's a former boyfriend?"

"I've only gone out with a few guys and only for fun, nothing serious."

"You need to be willing to give me their names Amy although I doubt it's any of these men. I think it's a woman who's after you Amy. It's someone you've had contact with and you must have upset them. Let's watch some television."

"Why don't we find a movie?"

"A good comedy, I need to get my mind off all of this for now."

After the movie There is something strange about Mary is over, "Ellen, let's sleep in this room with the two beds. "Okay Amy, I gather that Mike is sleeping in the master bedroom."

"He's hoping that if someone does find a way to break in without setting off the alarm or waking us up, that the un-sub will go to the master bedroom first unless the intruder mistakes Mike's snoring for a snarling guard dog."

Detective Goldstein wakes up to a sound of someone walking around downstairs. Could it be an intruder, the un-sub who is after her, or is she just hearing things and nothing is happening downstairs at all? Amy gets up and reaches for her gun and baton she carried when she was still on patrol. Walks towards the door of the room where she was sleeping to see if someone is really downstairs or is she just hearing things? Detective Goldstein wonders if it's just her partner making coffee. Amy walks slowly and notices that her sister is still sleeping, continues to walk towards her master bedroom when she notices that her partner and boyfriend Mike Fisher is not there. Amy is then relieved by the smell of coffee brewing. After all, what un-sub would break into someone's home and brew coffee. Well, if it turned out to be the un-sub, it would be like an episode from "Criminal Minds," or an episode from one of the CSI shows.

Detective Goldstein walks downstairs with caution and towards the kitchen, only to discover that it is only her partner and boyfriend Mike Fisher.

"I know my coffee is pretty bad, but you don't need to shoot me over it" he said putting his hands up. "I heard a noise and was beginning to think that someone had broken in until I smelled coffee brewing but still decided to use caution when coming downstairs."

"The first thing I did when I came downstairs was to glance out the window to see if someone was watching your house. Then, I decided to make some coffee knowing that you would want a cup when you woke up. If you glance outside every fifteen to twenty minutes you will notice that there is a bigger police presents. Amy, "Maybe you should consider taking a two week vacation?"

"I'm not going to take a vacation because someone might be after me. That's like running away."

"I was only suggesting you take a vacation Amy so you could get some rest."

"I don't need the rest Mike, I need to find out who is after me, and why."

"Why don't you just let me handle this along with the captain and Leon? "I'm not a little kid Mike."

"Once again Amy, I'm concerned for your safety."

"I'm not concerned for my safety Mike; I want to rip the heart out of the person who might want me off the force or dead."

"Amy, I believe the Chinese have a proverb"

"Before you embark on a journey of revenge, dig two graves."

Fisher's partner and girlfriend now awake. "Mike, would you ladies like some scrambled eggs and toast with tomatoes and green pepper?" Amy tells Mike, that she would try it. "What type of coffee did you make?"

"That's a surprise Amy. I brought some from my place. I thought you might like it." (It turns out that Fisher made Costa Rica Peaberry Coffee). "The biggest surprise will be if it doesn't kill me," she said. Ellen walks into the kitchen and says, "The smell of that coffee is incredible."

"That's the coffee I made. Its gourmet coffee"

"It looks like there is enough for the three of us."

"Absolutely Ellen, you can pour yourself a cup."

"Can you pour me a cup too Ellen, while I'm putting out the silverware?" While pouring a cup of coffee for both Amy and herself, Ellen asks Detective Fisher, "Do you have any ideas Mike who might be after my sister?"

"I'm working on that Ellen. I sent in a request via email and asked a favor of a friend of mine to check on someone regarding another case. This guy would have a motive but I'm not mentioning names right now."

"Why not"

"Because I don't want you searching for them via the Internet or using any connections you have and getting yourself in trouble."

"You think I'm out of control Mike?"

"No, Amy, but I don't want to see you become so obsessed that you can't think clearly. Amy, why don't you make a list of people you worked with after you left the academy."

"Mike, I think that's a poor use of time and energy. You said that you believe it's someone close to me like a family member, so you believe it's my sister who is after me right?"

CHAPTER 8

"Maybe the person who is after you is someone you arrested or you took the bust and upset another police officer? You know this is basic police work, Amy. So, get to work making a list of cops you worked with. Did you keep a journal or diary of people you arrested, officers you worked with early on in your career?"

"Mike, I did keep records of arrests I made and other officers I worked with on patrol. But why not just go through the standard system where all that information is kept? Come on Mike, you believe it's my sister so let's stop talking about other officers." In case we have a bad cop on duty, we don't want them to know there is an on-going investigation."

"Stop Mike, I still don't think it's a police officer or detective. My instincts tell me this is personal, Mike."

"No one is going to get hurt."

"Do you think it's safe for us to go outside and clean the snow off our cars?"

"Yes, Ellen, and I got some of the snow off my truck earlier when I went outside to get some fresh air and talk to a buddy of mine. He and his wife want us to come over on Christmas Eve for dinner. My friend and his wife do this every year. They have a big gathering of friends and family. Amy and I are going to my parent's home for the holidays. I usually take a gift for them and something for their kids but shortly before the holidays."

"That gets a bit expensive."

"Its not about what you spend for gifts Amy, it's the feeling you get from giving. Last year we all got together on Christmas day and served food that people donated to a shelter. A few police officers and a friend of mine from the FBI brought his family with him to help."

"Are you doing that this year, too?"

"No Amy, the shelter has plenty of people this year to serve dinners. Last year, they had lost three people so they were short handed."

"Did the three people move somewhere else?"

"No Ellen, they all lost their lives due to one illness or another. Let's go outside and clean the snow off our cars."

When they get outside Detective Fisher proceeds to look under the cars to see if there might be an explosive device. "Why did you look under our cars, Mike?"

"Just being cautious, Ellen."

"Ellen, don't let Mike fool you, he was looking for an explosive device and being our "knight in shining armor."

"That's so sweet; you and Mike should get married."

"I'm getting that feeling again Mike."

"You mean like someone is watching you?"

"Exactly Mike."

"Is it an eerie feeling Amy?"

"Yeah Ellen, that's exactly the feeling I'm getting."

"Start up your cars ladies and let them warm up."

"Did you hear what I said Mike?"

"Yes I did, Amy. Just let the car run for a little bit. You do the same with your car too Ellen."

While the ladies are cleaning off what's left of the snow on their cars, Detective Fisher is walking around the front of his partner's home. He's also going to have the two ladies shut off the engines to their cars. "Okay ladies, shut off the engines and lock up your cars. We are going to take a walk around the back of the house, pick up some wood for the fireplace and then go inside." After Fisher, Amy, and her sister Ellen pick up some wood, they do exactly what Fisher tells them to do. After leaving some wood on the floor near the fireplace, Fisher decides to go back outside to take another look around.

When he walks back into Amy's home, Fisher asks Amy, "Do you still have that tall ladder that reaches up to the spot light on the side of the house where the driveway is?"

"What are you going to do Mike?"

"I'm going to install two cameras I forgot I had left in my truck. The cameras have motion detectors and they will be mounted near where the light is, and the other I'm going to mount outside your front door."

"It's cold and icy out there today."

"Don't worry about it Ellen, Mike feels that our suspect is someone who is close to me, and Mike likes the cold. He's into cross country skiing."

While the two sisters watch some television, Detective Fisher runs some wiring he had in his truck so that he can setup the first camera above the spotlight so there is no glare, and then run the wiring into the house current. Detective Fisher is known for being quite knowledgeable when it comes to electrical work. He also sets up the wiring and mounts a camera so that anyone who comes near the front of the house is captured on video. Fisher decides not to mount the camera near the front door but mounts it in a corner of the front porch making it difficult for anyone to tamper with the camera. Fisher believes that if anyone is watching what he is doing, they can see that he is adding more security to protect his partner. Amy's sister now wonders if she is being considered a suspect. Detective Goldstein believes that it's only a matter of time before the un-sub and she meet. She's hoping to have a good shot off at this un-sub. Fisher is again wondering if it's someone close to his partner like her sister Ellen. Could it be someone she was once friends' with? Both cameras are mounted firmly and difficult to reach. Fisher knows that all he has to do is connect the wiring and install software in Amy's desktop computer and laptop, and then they can monitor any activity around the house. Detective Fisher walks in the front door, locks it behind him, and informs Amy and her sister that both cameras are mounted and he is going to connect them to the circuit box. "It's starting to snow again. If it clears tomorrow and it's not windy, I'll install another camera in the back of the house. Let me connect the wiring and then I can install the software on both your desktop and laptop computers."

"Can I use my cell phone to check on my house when I'm away from home Mike?"

"I believe the cameras I mounted with the security center in this box will allow you to do that."

"I want to see if these cameras show up on my cell phone."

Detective Fisher walks back into the living room, sits down at the desktop computer and installs the software for the camera security system. "According to what I'm reading here Amy, you have to download the application to this security system so it will work with your cell phone."

"Are there instructions for that?"

"Yes there are. I'll write down the website address and you can download the application from there."

"This still won't help us to catch this un-sub unless they show up and try to break in or walk around the front of the house."

"That may be true Amy, but this camera security system provides for more security while you are at home."

While Amy and her sister are watching television trying to get their minds off of this un-sub who is supposedly after Amy, Detective Fisher's phone rings and it's Agent Wolf from the FBI. "Is this Lenny?"

"This sure is Mike. You asked me a question about Mr. Thorn. He's not the guy you are looking for. He's not involved here."

"Well Lenny, that's one suspect out of the way."

"If it gives you any comfort Mike, in cases like this when its usually someone close. As you know, the Bureau uses victimology. We study the victim's lifestyle. Do you know what I'm trying to tell you Mike?"

"Yes Lenny, you want me to look closer at the people Amy knows, and what she does in her free time."

"That's correct. Do you need my assistance Mike?"

"Can you remain available?"

"Yes, I can Mike. Do you think Amy is in real danger?"

"I think it's a strong possibility and it's someone she knows."

"I'm trying to think of a way the Bureau could enter this investigation."

"I can't jump to conclusions Lenny. It's also up to my captain to ask the Bureau for its assistance."

"Do you want me to speak to Captain Costello about having the BAU join the investigation?"

"You and I both know that unless there is a series of homicides, rapes, or terrorist attacks, my captain or the chief won't invite the BAU into the investigation"

CHAPTER 9

"So Amy, I would like for you to know what I've been working on."

"I keep meaning to ask you what you are doing these days. Amy says to Ellen. "I just can't tell you, I have to take you to my place and show you one day."

"I know you were always good with figuring out cell phones and other electronics. Is that what your doing these days Ellen?"

"I'm doing more then that Amy. It's a surprise."

"Where is your shop Ellen?"

"I'll have you follow me there one day and show you what I've been working on."

"The way things are going my captain and his superiors are probably going to force me to take time off."

"Good. Then we can have lunch together and hang out."

"Agent Wolf told me that we should use victimology to help us catch this un-sub. Sometime in your past you may have made some boyfriend, or friend from school angry enough to comeback after you. I disagree Amy, but my friend Agent Wolf feels that we should use victimology to help us profile this un-sub."

"What do you think Mike?"

"I think it's someone really close to you Amy." "You mean someone I've been friends with most of my life?"

"Someone close"

"I'm trying to think Mike but nothing is coming to me."

"Give it some thought Amy, someone is after you and your life might depend on you remembering."

"A cousin"

"I remember telling someone I was friendly with as a teenager that we should go our separate ways because we started to fight more then we got along."

"This was a former boyfriend?"

"No Mike, this was a girlfriend. But she didn't seem angry at all when I told her that we should go our separate ways."

"Write down her name for me and address if you have it."

"Are you talking about Cathy?"

"Yeah Ellen, that's exactly who I was talking about."

"She was pissed at you. She just didn't say anything about it to you. She felt that you used her so you would have a place to hangout when you got into arguments with mom or dad. You didn't just upset Cathy you pissed her off. If anyone would have a grudge enough to make your life a living hell, it would be Cathy."

Detective Fisher isn't so sure about this woman Cathy. Fisher is a bit curious why Ellen would make such a statement but on the other hand Ellen isn't a trained investigator. Yes, this might all be quite personal rather then professional. Detective Fisher feels that if the person after Amy were a cop, they would have tried to hurt Amy in some way at this point but rather, nothing has happened. So, who is after Detective Fisher's partner, her sister, a brother, cousin, former classmate or a former friend?

At 8:00 PM Fisher gets a call on his cell phone and It's Captain Costello. The Captain tells Fisher that he and Leon have been trying to come up with a clue to who they believe is after Detective Goldstein. The captain tells Fisher that he and Leon looked at the personnel records of the officers who worked with Amy prior to her promotion. They only came up with one name and that officer would more likely go after Fisher then Goldstein.

"Captain, who do you think the officer with the grudge is?"

"Leon and I both considered Tamara. She was transferred and took a cut in pay."

"That was her own fault."

"Mike, this is true but how many people really take a look at themselves in the mirror, cops too. We ruled her out because she seems quite happy since she no longer works in our unit."

"So we are still dealing with an un-sub that is after Amy but we don't know the why, and how they are going to come after Amy, who they are, and where this might all occur? We are in essence, still in the dark. We are behind the 8 ball."

"I think there are some hidden clues that have been missed here. One of the questions you might ask yourself, who has easy access to Amy?" Detective Fisher standing by the front door asks, "Do you think it could be her sister? If so, why would her own sister want to harm her? Could we all be wrong about this Captain? No one has made any attempts to harm Amy at all."

"I asked myself those same questions Mike. If someone really wanted to hurt Amy, then why haven't they?"

"I've got some questions I failed to ask Amy and will get back to you if the answers are worth considering."

"Keep in touch Mike."

Fisher needs to speak to his partner and girlfriend but in private. He ponders how he can approach without insulting her sister. Fisher asks himself is the more direct approach better? He decides on the direct approach. Fisher, "Amy, you and I need to talk in private. Why don't we walk upstairs Amy? Fisher turns to Ellen and apologizes and tells her he needs to talk to Amy in private that its not like he doesn't trust her, It's a personal matter. The two friends as well as partners walk upstairs to the master bedroom where Detective Fisher must ask his partner and girlfriend some personal questions. Detective Fisher is hoping that these questions won't upset Amy, to whom he has come to love, to become angry with him to the point that she wants to end their relationship. Detective Fisher knows he has to ask questions and he starts with, "Amy, have you ever noticed if any of your under garments were missing from your home or where you lived in the past? Have you considered the possibility that it might be Ellen?"

"I never considered that it could be my sister."

"Mike, I've never had to deal with any of those things."

"Did you ever have a former boyfriend become aggressive with you to the point you had to use force?"

"No Mike. Are you going to ask me any questions that are more personal like how many guys I wanted to sleep with? I'll tell you, there have only been two. One guy had no interest in me, and the other guy is you. What are you trying to tell me Mike, that some guy really did want to sleep with me years ago but didn't want to have a relationship with me? I want to be with you Mike."

"I've been wanting for us to spend the entire night together for sometime, Amy. I love you and have been waiting for you to say yes. Lets wait until Ellen falls asleep Amy."

"You'll take it easy with me Mike?"

"You have my word Amy. May I ask Amy, why you changed your mind since you originally told me that you wanted for us to wait until we were married? It's not like we've never done the deed."

"But, it's different now, Mike. I've fallen in love with you. That wasn't love, this is love."

"Mike, you have been here for me despite that your life could be in danger as well. Your staying here with me has without words told me just how much I believe you love me. I want to share my life and love with you."

"Okay Amy. I'm going to take it easy with you. This should be a special night for both of us and especially for you."

"Lets wait until Ellen falls asleep. She had a couple glasses of wine and she won't be waking up at least until tomorrow morning. I told her to make sure to take a baby aspirin before she goes asleep this way she won't have such a bad hangover tomorrow morning."

"Good idea, and I bet you were more then willing to share your wine with her."

"Absolutely Mike."

"If you are going to use any birth control nothing but the pill okay. I have my reasons for this and I'm sure you can guess why."

"Are you saying what I think you are?"

"Yes Amy. I want all of you. This is the night I've been waiting for. You are so cute and in my eyes you will always be beautiful and these aren't just words, this comes from my heart." Amy, "Thank you Mike. I love you too and I want for us to make love tonight. Make me realize just how much you love me Mike."

The wine drinking caught up with Ellen and she is sleeping in the guest room. Amy walks into her bedroom where the man she has fallen in love with has been waiting for her with a blue robe and gray briefs on. Amy too, is wearing a red silk robe. Mike walks up to her slowly, brings her closer to him and then he begins to kiss her while he first lightly places his left hand on her right cheek and his right hand on her left arm slowly while they kiss, Amy with her right hand takes Mike's left hand and places it on her waist and then Mike takes his right hand off her left arm and slowly places his right hand on her hip on the left hand side of her body. Amy places her right hand on Mike's left hand side and then places her left hand on the robe and slowly pulls the robe open that Mike is wearing. Amy then rubs his chest. This will be a night of passion between Mike and Amy.

"I thought you wanted me to move slowly Amy, to take it easy with you?"

"That's true Mike. It's not like we are ripping each other's clothes off."

"I just want to make sure that I'm not becoming too aggressive with you. "You're not Mike. Actually, I'm quite excited so why don't we just make love to each other."

"Are you sure you are ready Amy?"

"I'm ready for almost anything we do together since I really love you Mike."

Amy and Mike get into bed when Mike tells Amy no under the covers yet. Mike and Amy move closer. His body touching hers and then he surprises her by getting on top continuing to kiss and make love to her. "Mike, are you really doing that?"

"Yes I am sweetheart."

"Are you ready for more dear?"

"Oh yes Mike." 60 minutes later Mike and Amy have made better love together then either one of them have had before. They both feel that they belong together."

"I love you Mike even more now then at anytime before this evening. Do you know why?"

"Why Amy?"

"Because you took your time with me." We've been sharing an intimate evening together."

"What's more beautiful then being intimate with the one you are in love with."

"That's right Amy. We have had more then most."

"I sure hope that our love for each other continues to grow. "Amy, I think everything will be just fine. We shared our love with each other tonight and that's something really special. It wasn't sex, it was love." Mike uses the remote control for the CD player Amy has in her room and turns on the song from the Phantom of the Opera, "All I ask of you."

"I've never been one for classical music or opera but that's the perfect song tonight."

"Glad you like it Amy. What a night this has been. It only makes me realize how much I really love you. I could see it in your eyes."

"Ellen is leaving in the morning. She told me that she has things to do but wants to get together with me next weekend. I'm going to take a shower Mike." May I join you Amy? "Pervert."

"I'm all yours Amy. You are my master tonight. "Are you serious. I'm your master and you're my male slave?"

"Yes Amy, I'm going to be your love slave tonight." Amy laughs, and says Wow, I love this!"

Amy and Mike are in bed and kiss. "Amy, you should spend sometime with your sister. Just make sure you let me know when you get together with her. Make sure you keep your cell phone on."

"Why Mike?"

"Because I think it's someone that you have been close to for years or from your past, who is after you."

The next morning after Fisher, Goldstein, and her sister Ellen had breakfast Ellen left to go back to her friend's place.

That night Mike and Amy make love together again. "Are you okay Amy?"

"Oh yes Mike, I can't believe you are doing this for me."

"That's because I love you Amy."

CHAPTER 10

WHAT HAPPENS NEXT?

The phone rings and Detective Goldstein answers the phone. "This is Captain Costello. How are you doing, Amy?"

"I'm doing great Captain."

"That's good Amy. Do you feel up to handling a missing person's case?"

"I'm up to it, Captain."

"If Mike is there tell him I need to see both of you at the office in an hour."

"I'll tell Mike and we'll be on our way."

"I'm almost dressed Amy."

"It will take me 15 minutes and then I'm ready to go."

"Fill me in Amy, what did the captain say?"

"He didn't say much. The captain just wanted to see us."

"I wonder if were dealing with a predator?"

"We could be working a big case Mike."

"If we are dealing with a predator, I want the captain to call my friend Lenny at the FBI and ask if he can assist us with the profile of our un-sub." What would be better then having the FBI assist us.

The two detectives get dressed, Amy sets her home alarm system and they stop off at a WAWA to pickup some coffee for the captain, Leon, Mike's own coffee and one for Amy. Mike and Amy pull up to the police department and take the elevator upstairs to meet up with Captain Costello. "Hello Leon got you and Captain Costello some coffee."

"Thanks Mike and Amy. The captain and I have some news for you and Amy, but Amy isn't going to like what we have to tell the both of you."

"What are you talking about?"

"Amy, we conducted a DMV check of all Subaru Outback wagons in this part of the state and only three matched up. Your sister's car was one of them." Unfortunately you or the officers were unable to get the license plate number. "Were still looking into the owners of the other two cars."

"Okay, so one of the cars belongs to my sister. But what have you learned about the other two owners? Do any of these other people have any connection with me?"

"That's why I wanted the both of you to come in to the office and look at the other names. Please tell me if you remember the name Cathy Somers?"

"Amy, didn't your sister Ellen say that you once had a friend named Cathy who is pissed off at you?"

"Cathy was angry with me for a short time but we've been friendly since."

"You didn't tell Ellen that when she mentioned that Cathy was angry with you that you and Cathy started talking again."

"I don't tell my sister everything Mike. Do you tell your family everything?"

"Of course not."

"How about you Captain Costello or you Leon. Do you tell your families everything?"

"You made your point Amy."

"Amy, we are only trying to learn who is after you. We are worried about your safety even though we know your pretty tough."

"You can't afford to let your guard down Amy."

"I know Captain; and I know you guys believe it's someone close to me." Leon, "I would keep in mind that it could be anyone. You might have even pissed off a family member who's been able to hide or control they're anger."

"Captain, have you called Lenny at the FBI and asked if he could send an agent to assist us with this situation?"

"I'll call Lenny before you start losing sleep over this."

"Now I know your busting my stones."

"Of course I am."

The captain laughs even more after he jokes with Detective Fisher. Fisher knows that the captain was only trying to make Fisher feel less tense. The three detectives and their captain have enjoyed cookouts and some holidays together. Mike Fisher has spent many holidays with Captain Costello's family.

"Seriously Captain, I'm running out of patience here. We need to come up with a profile on this un-sub and we could use Lenny's help."

"Absolutely Mike, I was just trying to take the edge off by making a joke. I know that Amy isn't as worried as you are Mike. Let me see if I can reach Lenny." The captain enters the phone number and a receptionist answers the phone, "FBI, how may I assist you?" The receptionist is Carol Duggan, a mother of two. Her husband Joe Duggan, a Federal Prosecutor, a tall husky guy whose height and build scares the crap out of any bad guys he's prosecuted. Her son Jerry performs threat analysis for the NSA, and her daughter Carla is a forensic science guru that reminds her co-workers of the character Abby in the original NCIS show with the loud music. Her daughter only goes to church once a year with the family and that's for Christmas Mass. Carla who could have become a member of any organization for people who are genius level laughed when someone asked her to join their organization. She told them that she didn't have any interests. Carla turned down a position in the lab with the FBI in Washington, D.C. to work for the NJ State Police and live closer to her family. Unlike the loyal to Gibbs character Abby in the show NCIS, Carla takes off for the Christmas holidays; and is only called in on a holiday if there is a series of crimes that are connected. Carla maybe called in to run DNA tests. The captain is able to reach Agent Wolf and ask him if he would be willing to assist the captain and his detectives with a profile of an un-sub whose been stalking Detective Goldstein. "Good afternoon Lenny, I'm calling because Mike, Leon, and I are concerned for Amy's safety. We believe she is being stalked by someone close to her, or someone she was once friendly with."

"You need to consider the people that Amy has had contact with that could hold a grudge. Do you believe her life is in danger as we speak or is someone just trying to harass her? I thought I gave you some insight into this un-sub earlier on, so you may want to check your notes Lou."

"I can't say for sure Lenny. That's why we called you again. If not for a profile today, I lost my notes from our last conversation."

"You are looking for someone who feels rejected in some way or someone who has an agenda and Amy is their target."

"I guess I'm staying at your place Mike."

In the back of her mind this couldn't be better. Amy wants to spend even more time with Mike since they made love together last night. Since becoming more interested in Mike and knowing his love for her, Amy started buying dresses or even skirts with classier looking blouses and women's suits for work that Mike has paid her with quite a few compliments. Amy left her hair a dark brown color and long. Although she doesn't put a lot of makeup on, she does use lip-gloss because she knows Mike likes it.

CHAPTER II

NO CLUE

"If you have any plans with family members, either I will be there with you, or you have to cancel them until this is all over. This includes the plans you had to get together with your sister. Now that Lenny is going to assist us with a profile of the un-sub Amy, we should follow his advice."

"Amy, this means you are on temporary but paid leave."

"You know Amy, you won't have a negative mark on your record."

"I know Captain. It really sucks that this un-sub is free to do what they want while I have to sit on the side line."

"We know you are pissed that you have to take time off Amy but this un-sub may try to kill or leave you permanently disabled. The captain and Agent Wolf are right. Use this time to take a trip somewhere and read a book on a beach or relax at home."

"Mike, you know Leon is right. You and Amy should plan a trip using under cover names and hang out on a beach."

"When you make plans, let us know but in person not by any other means."

"I have a place in mind for Amy and I to go."

"Hawaii Mike?"

"Not yet Amy."

"How about Hilton Head SC?"

"How about Orlando Florida Mike."

"Good idea. I have some friends and family down there. We could stay in a bungalow with the use of a private pool or we could go to Disney World and disappear in the crowds. I need to make a couple of phone calls."

Detective Fisher leaves Captain Costello's office to make some calls hoping Fisher will be successful in making travel arrangements that both Fisher and Amy, his partner and lover can live with. The problem is that if the un-sub is someone close to Amy, they might become angry when they see that Amy and Mike are taking a trip together. While Fisher is on the phone Detective Goldstein walks over and sits at her desk that is located only a few feet away from Detective Fisher's desk and to Fisher's left. When Detective Fisher hangs up he turns to his partner and tells Amy that they will have to wait at least four weeks. "That's no good Mike."

"So Amy, you stay with me." Amy is elated by what her lover and partner had to say. The thought of spending more time with Mike alone makes Amy feel warm inside. It's the image of last night that makes her feel this way. It's been a cold Wednesday afternoon and there is more snow in the weather forecasts for the northeast part of the country.

Another day in the department is over for Detectives Fisher, Goldstein, and Detective, Jackson. Captain Costello suggests that his detectives leave before the storm hits. Leon, "Well, if it snows, I'll be spending time with my family so if you need me for an emergency, you'll have to call me on my cell phone."

"No problem Leon, have a good time."

"I'm looking forward to spending time with my wife and sitting in front of the fireplace with a glass of wine or brandy."

"That sounds really nice captain."

"I have some wine back at my place Amy. We'll cook some dinner and try to enjoy the evening together."

"I'm looking forward to it Mike. Last night was really special for me."

"Being with you is always special for me. "Why don't we cook up some dinner and see what happens from there."

"I'm fine with that Mike."

The two detectives as well as lovers go back to Mike's home. Like his partner, Fisher too, owns a hot tub Jacuzzi. The two lovers use the hot tub. He enjoys cooking and his kitchen reflects this. He has a fairly large kitchen with a round handmade mahogany table that allows for 6 chairs for those times when Mike Fisher gets together with friends for a night of poker. In his Kitchen there is a top of the line Sharp Carousel counter microwave convection oven, a blender you would find behind a bar, a gas range with a traditional oven, and near his cooking appliances is an island where he can make salads, carve a turkey or chicken. The size of the island makes it easy for he and Amy to eat at the island rather then using the kitchen table. His kitchen walls are white with yellow borders where the ceiling and walls meet. The kitchen cabinets are a mustard color with white knobs and the wood-work around the cabinets are also white. The floor is a dark color brown with a rough finish to prevent slipping. The kitchen was done in French style.

Detective Fisher still laughs when officers or even strangers approach and tell him that he reminds them of the character from the Mike Hammer series of the 1970s. Detective Fisher always thanks people when they tell him so by saying, "What a compliment." Fisher was a big fan of the show himself.

CHAPTER 12

TIME TOGETHER

While Mike opens a bottle of white wine and places it in a bucket of ice for it to cool naturally, Mike takes out a salmon filet and uses some sauce he made up to season it. "I'll cook the fish up as one large filet and then cut it when it's done cooking Amy."

"Why are you putting the salmon in the microwave oven?"

"With this oven I can broil the fish and it comes out juicy not dry like fish can when you cook it in a traditional oven. I've cooked whole chickens and a duck in this oven."

"I put the silverware out and finished with the salad. What else can I help you with Mike?"

"Just relax Amy and I'll turn on some jazz if that's okay with you."

"Never been a big fan of jazz but maybe that's because I've only heard some jazz."

"I'll put on some "Smooth jazz." The two lovers have dinner together while the music plays in the background. After dinner Mike and Amy dance together.

Looking in each other's eyes Mike realizes that Amy wants for them to spend the rest of their lives together. "Mike, I can't tell you enough how much I love you and us being alone together. It means so much to me that we spend more time together like we did just last night. That was incredible. Some people would find it creepy or disgusting."

"Amy, do you know how much I want for us to spend the rest of our lives together. I think about it all the time. So what's the rush Amy, we just started dancing and you know that it's special when we move slowly and like the famous song goes, "We have all the time in the world." Who performed that song Mike?"

"Louie Armstrong." Mike gently pulls Amy closer to him and then begins to kiss her slowly. They begin to dance some more when Amy slips her shoes off. "Let's sit down on the sofa Amy and sip some wine together."

"Okay Mike. This is really good wine and I'm not sure if it's the wine or being with you and knowing how much we love each other is why I'm feeling so warm."

"Are you sure you want for us to spend another night together Amy?"

"Yes Mike."

"Why don't we use the bedroom Amy?"

"I would rather us sit and kiss right here on this nice soft leather sofa. Why did you decorate your living room like this?"

"Why do you ask Amy?"

"Because your kitchen is so bright and your living room just seems so different from the way you had your kitchen done, although, I like the black leather Mike."

"Glad you like it Amy, but lets not talk about this right now." Mike and Amy are kissing again. Let's take our time Amy. I love you and don't want for us to ruin something that can be so beautiful."

"I agree with you Mike but I'm not afraid that we will ruin our relationship."

Mike and Amy decide to kiss even more while on the sofa. Amy extends her arms out to hug Mike while they are kissing while lying back on the sofa.

CHAPTER 13

THE HOLIDAYS

While Amy and Mike are sleeping the snow has been falling due to a storm front that moved from the west and shifted east in addition to a storm front what started in North Carolina and moved up the east coast. By the time the storm would come to an end, the northeastern part of the country would be dealing with feet, not inches of snow. When Mike wakes up, he puts on his robe and walks to the kitchen to turn on the coffee maker, he hears what sounds like a snowplow, walks to the front door and peaks out to see what is probably two feet of snow. Mike thinks to himself that this is going to be some holiday season. Mike may have been raised Jewish but his parents and grandparents wanted for Mike, his sister Beth, and brother Ben, while as children, to appreciate and respect both Christian and Jewish holidays.

The aroma from the coffee brewing wakes Amy up. She too puts on her robe over the pajamas she is wearing and walks into the living room and sees Mike looking out the window. "Good morning Mike. What are you looking at?"

"Good morning Amy. Why don't you come over and take a look outside."

"Wow! How much snow do you think we got last night?"

"I bet two feet. We're going to have a White Christmas. Wait until you spend sometime with my family and their neighbors. There is lots of food and anything you want to drink, plus desserts."

"I've never celebrated Christmas Mike. You know I have a father who is religious and we didn't celebrate Christian holidays like Christmas."

"Don't worry about it. Just have fun. I already finished shopping for the Christmas holidays weeks ago. We are going to have lots of fun. Trust me."

"I thought you were going to put up a tree in your house?"

"We are both going to setup the tree right over there. I already strung lights on the bushes outside this window and even if you look at the pole at the end of the driveway, you can see I strung lights on that too. I do it every year."

"Are you sure you're Jewish Mike?" Amy is smiling almost to the point of laughing. "Yeah Amy, I'm Jewish. My sister, brother, and I were raised as reform." With a smile on his face Mike tells Amy, my sister brother, and I even did the Bar and Bat Mitzvah thing."

"I guess were staying here for awhile Mike."

"You're fine with that, aren't you Amy?"

"Yes I am Mike."

"Good Amy. After breakfast I have to plow out the driveway and sidewalk. You're going to stay in the house Amy."

Mike and Amy have a couple of eggs and toast with coffee, rinse their dishes off and place them in the dishwasher. Shortly after that Mike and Amy both get dressed and Mike goes out to his garage to start the snowplow. While Mike is outside using the plow to clear the driveway and sidewalk, Amy's cell phone rings. She looks at the phone to see who is calling. Amy thinks for just a few seconds wondering who is calling and answers the phone.

"Who is it?"

"This is Ellen, can you believe this storm we got. Never seen anything like it. We should get together soon Amy. I have something to show you. I've been working on a project but want to surprise you. Let's make plans to get together next week, okay?"

"Sounds like a plan Ellen."

"Good Amy, can't wait to share with you what I've been working on and it's our secret Amy, okay?"

"Okay Ellen." Shortly after ending the call, Amy wonders why Ellen won't even give her a hint.

Mike is done using the snowplow and comes back into the house and realizes that Amy is upset about something. "What's wrong Amy?"

"Ellen just called and wants for us to get together next week. She told me that she has been working on a project Mike and asks me not to tell anyone."

"I'm sure its nothing Amy."

"I'm beginning to wonder if the captain and Leon are right."

A few days go by and Ellen calls to ask Amy if she wants to get together. Amy tells her sister that She and Mike are going to visit some of his relatives and would like to have lunch or dinner together. Ellen tells Amy "That's okay Amy, we can get together after your visit with Mike's family."

"Thanks Ellen for being patient with me. I look forward to our time together. "What you need Amy is to get your mind off the person who is after you. Why don't you help me put up the Christmas tree? I know you haven't done this before so we'll do this together. I'll turn on some music while we put the lights on the tree. "So you like different color lights not just the white lights."

"I think white lights belong in stores or public places not at or in someone's home. I think white lights are for commercial use. This is what we are going to do. I'm going to put the lights on here, pass them on to you so that you can lay the lights around the other side of the tree, I always start from the bottom of the tree and do a row at a time until I get to the top of the tree. "Then what do we do?" After all the lights are on the tree and as you can see they are working, then comes the garland, followed by the ornaments like these color balls in that box. I even have a star for the top of the tree. I hope it's at least a Jewish star."

"Actually Amy, I do have a Jewish star for the top of the tree. I had it made special. Are you feeling any better that we are doing this together?"

"Yes I am Mike."

"Wait until we are done decorating the tree and the room is dark except for the lights on the tree."

The house phone rings and Mike answers it. Mike, "Who's calling?" The person calling Mike Fisher is his mother Sarah. Fisher's mother is thin build, a brunette, and has been a hair stylist for 40 years and is often complimented for how young she looks for her age. Never smoked anything, likes to drink red wine a few times a week with dinner or at family gatherings. Fisher's father is a retired Marine and FBI agent. Joseph Fisher wanted Mike to become an FBI agent but Mike didn't want to live in Texas or any of the southern states the FBI told him he would have to relocate to in order to work for the Bureau. His sister Beth is a GP or family doctor. She is single. Fisher's brother is an attorney who started out as a federal prosecutor who was then offered position with a well-respected law firm. Benjamin Fisher took courses to become a certified trial attorney and at times he defends doctors in malpractice cases. Most of the time he does corporate law, disability related cases, and some divorce law. Mike's mother tells her son that everyone is getting together on Friday evening at 6:00 PM. She asks Mike if Amy will join them for dinner. Mike lets his mother know that Amy is coming with him.

"Mom, Amy was raised in a religious household. This will be Amy's first time celebrating the holiday season like our family has for years. I think this will be good for Amy. She's been dealing with a lot of stress lately since someone's been giving her a difficult time." Sarah, "We'll make her feel right at home. Do you realize Mike that we haven't seen a "White Christmas" in years like the one we are having this year. Your father said he will use the snow to keep some of the bottled drinks cold since we don't have enough ice."

"Why not, it beats going out to the store for bags of ice or taking up a lot of space in the refrigerator that can be used to keep the food fresh."

"We will see you at 6:00 on Friday, just two days away Mike."

"I've been looking forward to it Mom."

Mike gets off the phone, "Amy my family can't wait to have you over for the holiday party Friday night. So lets have some fun setting up this tree. So now that we have the lights on your tree and they are all working, what do we do next? "Amy, we put the garland on the tree. I use silver and gold garland. It's like an old song that was used in a Christmas cartoon"

"I think I've seen that cartoon but don't remember the song."

"How can you forget that song? Burl Ives performed that song, a famous actor. Did you know Amy that some of the best Christmas music and cartoons were written and produced by Jewish people? The music for the movie "White Christmas," was written by Irving Berlin, a Jewish guy."

"Okay Mike, how do we put the garland on the tree?"

"We'll do it together.

I'll start the garland and pass it over to you. You'll lay it on the branches and pass it back to me."

"Why are we starting from the bottom and going up the tree?"

"That's just the way I've been putting the garland on the tree for years. Are you okay with the music Amy?"

"Yes Mike, its fine."

The two lovers decide to spend a quiet evening watching some television with the tree setup and only the lights on the tree are lit. They're both tired and go to sleep early. The next morning Mike gets up and goes downstairs to make some coffee and read the news on the Internet using his laptop. As far as Fisher is concerned, the best way to get the news is on the Internet. He does have a newspaper delivered but can't stand the liberal media on television. One sided news reporting. Fisher gets off the sofa, goes in the kitchen and pours himself a cup of coffee, adds a little sugar and creamer and goes back to the sofa and goes to the site of the Wall Street Journal. Fisher likes the journal because it's a more balanced resource of news for him.

After reading the Journal, Mike decides to type in local news for Egg Harbor Township New Jersey to see if anything interesting shows up. What pops up on his monitor is an article involving a Subaru Outback Wagon that looks similar to the one Mike, the captain, and Leon were looking for. As he looks more closely he realizes it's not the same car and that means there are only two owners Mike, his boss, and his peers need to consider including Amy's sister. Mike feels he is getting closer to the un-sub and closing this case, but is he right?

Amy walks out of the room and sees Mike on the sofa using the Internet. "Good morning Mike, what are you doing?"

"I've been reading news articles and found an article that a Subaru Outback was in an accident in our area. It wasn't your sister so don't worry about that. After reading the article Amy, it made me wonder if your sister Ellen is our un-sub. Just think about the possibility Amy. She does own the same model and color that we have been looking for."

"Why would my sister be after me Mike, she is intelligent, successful in her own right, and were close?"

"People change Amy. She might be angry and yet, she has been keeping her anger inside. There could be a number of reasons why Ellen might be doing this. If she calls again and wants for the both of you to get together, then lets make sure we put a plan in place. Let's make sure that we put a tracer device on you, or better yet, have you swallow a capsule that will allow the captain, Leon, and I to follow the both of you from a distance."

"I can't believe my sister would do anything to hurt me like this."

"Amy, call your sister tomorrow and ask her when she wants to get together. I hope I'm wrong Amy, but my gut instinct is telling me that your sister is involved to some extent."

"I can't believe my sister would do anything like this."

"I said its possible, just look at what we have to go on. A Subaru Outback wagon, that is the same color and body style as the car that you saw driving away. Two patrol officers witnessed the same type of car parked down the street but with a clear view of your home; and a young attractive lady with brown hair sitting in the car."

"Why didn't those officers stop to check this woman out if she was just sitting in her car?"

"I think Leon and the captain asked the same question. They were told that the woman appeared as though she might have been warming up her car. That she either lived in one of the houses or was visiting someone and getting ready to leave. People are allowed to let their cars run for awhile before driving off Amy."

"I just can't understand why my own sister would do anything to hurt me."

"I'm sure we'll learn why. Lets go out and get something to eat at Bartucci's."

"I thought it wasn't a good idea for me to go out in public."

"You're not going out alone or with anyone else Amy, you're going to be with me."

"Okay, let's go, I'm ready."

It's Wednesday night and the two lovers decide to go out to Bartucci's Restaurant to have dinner rather then stay inside another night. They arrive at the restaurant and they each decide to order a vodka martini chilled. "Why don't we each get something different and share."

"Sounds good to me. I'll get the chicken Caesar Wraps."

"I'll try their new Salmon platter, both sound like healthy meals."

"I can imagine what we'll be eating on Friday night when we get together with your family."

"We'll have salad, Chicken or turkey, stuffing, I'm sure one of the neighbors will either bring ribs or sausage over along with some potato salad. Don't worry Amy; they won't be offended if you don't eat any sausage. My sister doesn't eat sausage. The desserts usually include the choice of home made chocolate rum balls and chocolate chip cookies, sugar cookies, some fruit, a fruitcake, and like you, my sister likes yogurt, and so you'll have a choice of strawberry, blueberry, or even yogurt made with bananas. One year my mother baked a raspberry cheesecake. That was excellent. Maybe she made another cheesecake?"

While at Bartucci's Restaurant, Amy asks her lover and partner if he feels as though someone is watching them. Fisher responds, "Amy, I think were safe here. It doesn't look to me that anyone is watching us. Are you okay?"

"Yeah Mike, I just got this strange feeling but now I feel better." With a smile on Mike's face, he tells Amy, "I don't see your sister here so I believe "The coast is clear." With a startled look on her face Amy replies, "Very funny Mike."

"A little humor never hurts."

A few minutes later a gentleman walks up to the two detectives and introduces himself to the detectives as Daniel Powel and Amy who asks abruptly for Powel to please leave that they are having dinner. Mike Fisher for the first time sees another sign of Amy that he finds cold and he seems to feel as though a sign of penned up anger. This behavior on the part of Amy concerns Mike. He begins to ask himself if its time for him to look into medical records on Amy's past. For now, Mike Fisher will hope that the two of them have a nice dinner together. Maybe this guy upset her in the past and she just doesn't want to have anything to do with him? Could this guy be a suspect? Could this guy be the one who is after her Mike wonders? Maybe he is wrong about her sister? Mike and Amy place their order with a waitress that looks Mike over but not to catch Amy's attention. The Waitress, Bonnie Fine, finds herself attracted to Mike Fisher. She is an attractive lady who is 24 years old with long, dark brown hair and brown eyes. Mike senses that this waitress likes him but doesn't want Amy to realize this. In the back of his mind he doesn't rule out the idea of becoming friends with her if things don't work out with Amy. He's only seen Amy act rude once before since he's met and gotten to know her. That was when they were working on the last case, The Paraffin Glove.

Mike and Amy are sharing and eating dinner when Mike looks up and there is Amy's sister Ellen with a young man. She smiles at Mike but doesn't walk over to their table. "Amy, your sister just walked in the restaurant with a young man and sat over in the far corner from us."

"You're kidding Mike. She didn't even come over and say hello."

"Maybe she is out on a date or doesn't want to disturb us while we are having our dinner?"

Once again, Amy doesn't seem to be acting right for someone in her age range or the position she holds. Mike is becoming even more concerned with Amy's behavior. To Mike, something doesn't seem right or maybe he is just getting tired. "Did that guy hurt you when you were younger?"

"That was in my past and no Mike, he wouldn't come after me."

"Okay."

Mike and Amy have finished dinner, paid the check and left the restaurant without Amy walking over to her sister since Amy didn't want to interfere with Ellen's dinner date. Mike and Amy get into Mike's truck and drive back to Mike's place. Amy has a feeling that Mike is keeping something to himself, but what is it? Does he feel that Amy is hiding something from him about her past? A long time ago when Amy was younger, she being one of the oldest of five children had to deal with a terrible divorce between her parents. Although it took years, Amy came to terms with the ordeal and went on with her life. She is after all, a very intelligent person who came to realize that despite what her father had to say about her mother was wrong and not true. Amy has become a well-respected and successful detective. She has worked on and solved some tough cases and even received two awards. Now she is facing an adversary that could be someone who is close to her. Amy has been having these same thoughts over and over again since this all began.

The next day Amy's sister calls her and Amy tells Ellen that after she has dinner with Mike and his family she will get together with her sister and see what her sister is up to. Amy is wondering what could Ellen be up to or have discovered? She knows her sister is quite brilliant and knowing Ellen, Amy figures Ellen discovered something that could save the lives of many people or turn the world of science or technology upside down.

The following morning while Mike and Amy are having breakfast, Mike asked Amy not to discuss anything to do with this case that he doesn't want his family to worry about their safety. Amy doesn't tell Mike that she heard from her sister and that they are getting together soon. Amy senses something is wrong between she and Mike but she is probably wrong. Sometime after Mike and Amy get back to his place after dinner, Mike gets a phone call and its Detective Jackson.

"How are you doing Leon?"

"I'm okay but I'm not sure how you are going to feel about the information I'm going to share with you."

"Tell me Leon."

"I did some interviewing and ten people told me that Amy has had some issues with some people in the past and the captain does know about it."

"What did the Captain have to say?"

"He said that he and the chief of police are going to give Amy the opportunity to take medical leave that she has saved up. She might be able to return to her position in a couple of weeks. She has been an excellent detective and the bosses don't want to lose her but it's time to make changes in our department."

Both Mike and Amy go to sleep early on Thursday evening. Friday will be a long day. Mike and Amy will spend time with Mike's family and their neighbors. It's going to be a "White Christmas." They read the newspaper, use the Internet to check their emails and delete what they don't need anymore. When Amy falls asleep while reading, Mike leaves the room to go in his study to watch a football game and do some reading. Fisher wonders what the un-sub is planning. He's thinking of asking her why she can't put the past to sleep. Mike has two clocks that make sounds every 30 minutes and on the hour. When he hears the clock at 4:00 PM on Friday, he stands up, walks out of his study and into the living room to see if Amy is awake. She is still sleeping so he speaks in a soft voice calling her name and she wakes up. "Amy, we should start getting ready to go to my parents home for dinner. I'm sure you'll have a good time."

"I brought a dress and I also have a nice pants outfit with me. Do you think I should wear the dress?"

"Show me the dress you're talking about."

"I'll get it and show it to you." A few minutes goes by and then Amy walks into the living room where Mike is sitting and Amy asks Mike, "Do you prefer the dress or the pants outfit?"

"Amy, I prefer the dress rather then the pants outfit."

"Mike, can you ask your mother what most of the women will be wearing?"

"Take my word for it, okay."

"I'll wear the dress Mike, no big deal."

"Lets start getting ready for the party. Take your time Amy we don't have to be there until 6:00 PM. I'm sure you will have a good time tonight. After tonight you and I should sit down and talk."

"You don't want to sit down and talk right now?"

"No Amy,

I want for us to have a good time tonight and have a serious conversation tomorrow. Nothing bad Amy"

"You know or learned something recently and your afraid I'll let anything you know ruin my time with your family."

"I think we should enjoy the evening and talk about the case tomorrow."

"Okay." Prior to first becoming a police officer then promoted to the rank of detective, Amy's interest was in psychology. She wanted to help kids who came from broken families. Her career as a detective could be put on hold after the holidays if anything else happens that makes her superiors nervous about Amy's behavior since first telling her partner Mike Fisher, that Amy thought someone was watching her.

It's Christmas Eve. Mike asks Amy to help him put some packages in his truck. "I'm glad to be of help to you?"

"Don't worry about it Amy, I signed the cards from the both of us."

"Your too much Mike."

"Yes, I've been told that before."

After loading up Mike's truck, Mike and Amy drive over to where Mike's family lives. You wouldn't believe that Mike came from a Jewish family seeing the front lawn decorated for the Christmas holiday. There is even a Santa, reindeer and sleigh setup on the roof of the house." His father decorates because he enjoys doing so.

Amy, with a smile on her face almost to the extent of laughing asks Mike if he is sure he's Jewish. Mike responds to Amy telling her with a smile on his face that yes, my family is Jewish. "Christmas isn't just about giving or receiving gifts or parties, it's about being with those you love, sharing with those less fortunate, and who says someone has to be a Christian to enjoy the season."

Mike and Amy arrive at the home of Mike's family shaking hands and hugging one another. Mike asks his brother Ben if he would help him take the presents he and Amy brought, out of his truck. Mike comes from a close family. While outside getting the presents out of the truck Ben compliments his brother after meeting Amy.

"Mike, Amy is not only attractive but cute. She seems like she is an intelligent person as well. What's she like as a detective?"

"Amy is an excellent detective but between you and I there is a possibility she may not be a detective much longer."

"Why Mike, what did she do?"

"She might need your help Ben. You're an attorney with lots of connections and she might need the connections you have."

"Is she going to face criminal charges?"

"No. I think she is actually going to be offered a position as a police psychologist but she might need your help to make sure the benefits she presently has are not terminated. Becoming a police psychologist will change her status with the police department."

"You want to make sure she keeps her present benefit package?"

"That's correct."

"Amy doesn't know anything about this as of yet, so we are not going to mention anything to her. "I understand. No plans are actually in place yet. But maybe I'll have to assist her in developing a new contract?"

"That's correct Ben. All this is being discussed between the Police Commissioner, our new police chief, and Captain Costello."

"Well, we're all here to have a good time with family and friends. Mike, do you need me to help you with that bag?"

"No."

"By the way Mike, do you know that we have a new Commissioner of Public Safety?"

"No I didn't."

"Yes Mike, we do. Sharon Miller took the oath of office this morning. Are you sure you are okay carrying that bag of gifts?"

"I got it Ben."

"It looks like more snow is on the way Mike."

"That's global warming for you."

The two brothers laugh, Mike closes the hatch on his truck and they walk back into the house where they grew up. "You guys were outside for awhile."

"We were getting the presents out the truck Amy and Ben was saying that we are suppose to get more snow."

"How much snow?"

"I heard three to six inches. That means we will end up with thirty inches by the time the snow stops."

Al Sandler, a close friend and neighbor for years, "I remember when we had snow every year at this time and sometimes up to ten inches. We use to build fortes and have snowball fights." While the guys were talking snowball fights and the times when they played hockey, the ladies were relaxing with mixed drinks and talking about investing in the stock market and new designer wear. Mike's mother was telling the other ladies how she was glad she didn't sell her Exxon Oil or shares in Microsoft. She was also telling the other ladies about a pocketbook and dress she saw the other day. Amy sat and listened. Sarah Fisher has money in mutual funds and bonds a friend told her about some years ago. When the timer goes off in the kitchen Mike's mother and aunt Judy take some of the food out of the oven and place it on the dining room table. The ladies tell everyone its time for dinner. While at the dinner table Mike's family, friends, and Amy talk about the weather, and restaurants they like. Everyone agrees that the movies that are out haven't been so good for the prices charged to see them.

"It seems that most of the action movies are based on the same kind of violence we see on the news, and movies that are advertised as romantic leave nothing for imagination. Within an hour into these movies couples are in bed together." Al the neighbor from next- door, "Even the horror movies that have come out are the same old thing."

"That's right, I forgot you like horror movies Al. Didn't you write a book and have it published?" Al, "Yes Mike, I had my book published and it has done well. They killed my entire family." (No such book written or published as far as this author knows).

After dinner everyone helps to clean up and goes into the living room where they exchange and open presents prior to leaving since the weather forecasters are calling for another storm that could dump another six to twelve inches of snow rather then just three to six inches.

After everyone has received, opened and gave thanks for the evening spent with Mike's family, Mike and Amy put their presents in Mike's truck, then they help Ben and his wife Julie with their presents and head home.

It's 10:00 PM when Mike and Amy return to Mike's place and the snow starts to fall.

"Well, here comes another snow storm according to my brother Ben. I guess you will be staying here with me at least another day Amy."

"I have no problem with that." The two lovers spend another night together and both go to sleep shortly afterwards. Captain Costello asks the chief if Amy can be moved into her new position sooner. Captain Costello tells Mike "Amy is going to be offered a position as a staff psychologist. It's a different kind of promotion, but I don't want you to talk to her about it. I'm not sure of what the commissioner or chief has in mind. We are all being kept in the dark of any decisions made by the commissioner or the chief. So take this time to enjoy the weekend off and keep an eye on her. I have a feeling that Amy was right, that someone has been watching Amy and might have plans to hurt her."

"Once again Captain, do you think its someone close to her like her sister?"

"I think that's a possibility. I don't think it's a stranger or someone she arrested in the past."

"We really don't have any evidence or a right to stop her from getting together with her sister or any other family member."

"If she tells you that she wants to get together with her sister, ask her to please consider the weather outside, its pretty bad out there and Governor Christi called for a state of emergency. He doesn't want anyone on the roads unless it's an emergency. You can use that as a reason for her to stay at your place at least until Monday."

"I'll tell Amy that the governor doesn't want anyone on the roads at this time."

"That's a good idea just to keep her there at your place."

"You know Amy as well as I do, when she makes a decision she does what she wants."

Later in the morning, Mike goes out to his garage to start the snowplow and plow the snow out of the driveway and then the sidewalk for the second time in just two days. While he is outside, once again, Amy gets a call from her sister to see when the two of them can get together so her sister can show Amy what she has been up to. "I haven't been avoiding you Ellen. My superiors don't want me going anywhere or with anyone until they can learn who has been watching me."

"Your superiors have no right to keep you from hanging out with me."

"They are following procedures Ellen."

The door opens and Amy hears Mike coming in so she tells her sister they will talk later and make plans to get together. Her sister ends the call and waits in anticipation for when she and her sister get together. This is when Ellen will take her sister to what use to be a warehouse where Ellen will take Amy on a tour. But what's in the building and what is Amy's sister doing there?

It's Sunday morning and Saturday was just a day for the two lovers to just rest. Mike and Amy wake up to another snowfall but not as bad as originally believed by weather forecasters. The phone rings; at Mike's home and Mike is informed by Captain Costello that a meeting has been setup for he and Amy to attend on Monday morning.

"Good morning Amy, How are you doing this morning?"

"I'm fine Mike, how are you doing this morning? Looks like were going to have another day together."

Mike with a smile on his face responds, "Are you hinting at something?"

"What do you think?"

"I think we should wait awhile. I have to submit a report to the captain Amy, you know that it's standard procedure even when it's been quiet." Nothing happens between the two lovers. What Mike doesn't know is that Amy has been talking with her sister and making plans to have lunch together and see what her sister has been up to. Amy's phone rings and it's her sister. "Can you talk now?"

"Yes, Mike went into his study to write up a report. When do you want to get together, it has to be sometime during the weekend when I can go home."

"How about Saturday?"

"That might work, let's see what happens between now and then."

Monday December 27th, 10:00 AM, Mike and Amy are called into the meeting Mike was confidentially told about. In the Conference room is the new secretary to the commissioner Barbara Shore, another new chief of police who was chosen to replace the last chief who was suppose to take over. Chief Frank Dudley's personality is more laid back and holds degrees from MIT and

LaSalle University in Philadelphia, Pennsylvania in Behavior Analysis, and Computer Science. Chief Stone left to go back to work at the FBI.

"Amy, I've been reading over your file and went back to look at the arrests you've made since joining the police department. I read over your application and looked at the results of the exam you took in order to become a police officer and then promoted to the rank of detective. I was impressed by what I read, but something caught my eye regarding your application and I decided to look into your past, and I was even more impressed that you did everything you could to deal with any frustrations you had as a child and with your degree in psychology, I want for you to become the psychologist for the police department. Your duties will change and if you choose, you won't have to wear slacks or pants suits any longer. It's your choice. As your new chief I haven't decided if we will require you to carry a side arm. I'm going to be perfectly honest with you Amy, this is going to be the toughest job you probably ever held."

"So you want me to be a staff consultant for the police department when it comes to people under investigation for violent crimes?"

"Yes I do."

"Good Amy. If you're okay with all this we can conclude this meeting."

"Commissioner Miller I have a question to ask."

"Go ahead Mike, what do you want to ask."

"Does Amy keep the benefits she already has even though she will become the psychologist for the department?"

"I'm pretty sure Amy that you will keep the benefits you already have with the department."

"Thank you Commissioner Miller."

After the meeting is over Amy asks Mike, "You were worried I was going to lose the benefits I have Mike. Thank you, that was really thoughtful of you."

"I'm glad you're not upset with me for asking." Monday evening December 27th, Amy is able to return to her own home. Her cell phone rings and its her sister. "Hi Amy, where are you?"

"I'm at home Ellen."

"Is everything okay between you and Mike?"

"Everything is fine as far as I know. Mike and I were called into a meeting with the new Commissioner of Public Safety for Egg Harbor Twp."

"What happened Amy?" I was promoted today. The New commissioner and chief of police want me to become the psychologist for the department."

"That's great Amy. We should go out and celebrate. What day is good for you?"

"Is this Saturday still good for you?"

"That's perfect for me. I don't always work on the weekends. Do you want to get together for lunch?"

"That's fine. Where do you want to meet?"

"Giovanni's Best of Italy."

"How about 12:30 Ellen, is that okay with you?"

"That's fine, we'll meet then."

For days its quiet at police headquarters when a call comes in. A woman is found raped and murdered. She is 24 years old and a brunette. The person who killed her must have been in a hurry to get rid of her body because a jogger didn't just find her remains, but also found her pocketbook in a bush right near the woman's body. Shortly after arriving at the scene Detective Fisher notices something odd, the un-sub didn't just dump her body they made it look as though they placed her body with remorse. At the scene is jogger Mary Sanders, the new coroner's assistant Gary Moran, and Mike Fisher.

"Do you have an idea for the T.O.D. (Time of Death)?"

"I'd say based on the temperature of the body this woman has been dead for six hours. We'll learn more after we get her back to the lab."

"Thank you Gary. The way this woman's remains were left here after the un-sub killed her reminds me of another case I worked years ago."

Captain Costello arrives at the scene and when he sees the woman he turns pale white as though he knows her but doesn't. He too, remembers a case he and Detective Fisher worked just a few years ago.

"Do you remember the last time we worked a case similar to this Mike?"

"We never caught the un-sub even with the help of the FBI and the Behavioral Analysis Unit. If this is the same un-sub we are going to find this un-sub and bring them to justice."

"Leon, take as many photos of this scene as you can. Try not to miss any angles, I think our un-sub is the same sexual predator Mike and I dealt with before. I want this scumbag."

"I want to call Amy and let her know we could have another serial killer on our hands.

They aren't going to stop this time unless we catch them. Were going to need her to study the photos with us and see if we can all develop a profile based on this homicide and the case we handled years ago with the FBI."

"Are you going to put a call into Lenny Wolf?"

"Yeah Mike, we have a responsibility to the public to ask the FBI to help us with this case."

"Good."

"I'm sure the FBI will want to get involved with this investigation. They want this un-sub too."

Amy receives a phone call from Mike that there has been a rape and homicide. He tells her that he and Captain Costello believe it's a sexual predator they and the FBI tried to catch a few years back but the un-sub is extremely intelligent and leaves no bodily fluids or prints behind. The predator is very organized. They tell Amy they are on their way back to police headquarters and to please wait for them to return. "Hi Amy, Captain Costello will be up here soon. Leon took photos of the victim from all angles and we already learned that she died a little over 6 hours ago. Our un- sub must have kept her for at least a day before leaving her body to be found. The Captain is talking with the chief and FBI to see if it's okay to release a description of the victim to the press hoping that someone saw something."

"We are hoping that by showing you photos of this victim and other women who were murdered a few years back, that you might be able to give us some insight into why the un-sub has picked these women. "This predator may have picked these women that remind them of people who rejected them. Most predators just want to have power over their victims. I believe that other predators look for women who remind them of their mother, or aunt, or a girl who were abusive or rejected them. Of course this isn't my area of expertise. I think we should ask the FBI to assist us with this investigation. The FBI agents with the Behavior Analysis Unit have expertise in building profiles of un-subs."

"Let's talk with the captain and ask if he already called the FBI. I believe he was going to ask the chief and Commissioner Miller for their permission to ask the BAU to assist us with this investigation."

The phone rings in Captain Costello's office and another woman has been found dead in her backyard. This woman wasn't just dumped like the last victim or previous victims. Captain Costello hangs up the phone and calls he and Mike Fisher's friend, Agent Lenny Wolf in Trenton. "Is Special Agent Wolf in his office today?" The operator, Julie Fields, "Yes he is. To whom may I ask is calling?" This is Captain Costello of the Egg Harbor Police Department, and I need to speak to Agent Wolf, it's serious." Ms. Fields, "I'll put you through to his office."

Special Agent Wolf is in his office when the phone rings and its Captain Costello. Agent Wolf, "Hello Lou! What can I do for you today?"

"We have two women found murdered in a similar fashion as the victims a few years ago."

"You think it's the same un-sub we've been looking for the past few years?"

"Yes we do."

"Whose the lead investigator on this case?"

"I put Mike Fisher in charge and one of our new detectives Leon Jackson. They're both excellent investigators but my superiors and Mike Fisher were asking if the BAU would assist us in this investigation."

"So Lou, you are inviting the BAU into this investigation?"

"I thought the Bureau would want to be involved in this investigation. This guy got away last time and the press bashed all of us."

"Lou, I was just busting your stones. Of course the Bureau wants to be involved in this investigation. Your department can take the lead and the BAU will assist you."

"You know my friend, I don't mind sharing the credit with the Bureau as long as we can catch this psychopath."

"We won't worry about that now Lou."

"This psychopath has always been one step ahead of us."

"This time we are going to get him."

"Lenny, this psycho has to prove that they have no fear of us. Killing his last victim in her own home and leaving her remains in her own backyard makes me believe that he is becoming more aggressive."

"Lou, this un-sub might only be looking for attention. I believe, he might even be asking us to catch him without saying so. Ted Bundy knew what he was doing was wrong but he would have kept killing girls if he hadn't got caught. We don't want to get this un-sub angry, we don't want to challenge him. Not yet. I'm pretty sure that the BAU will assist you with this investigation. Even if they are busy handling another case, I'll assist you with this investigation and call a couple of retired FBI agents who were with the BAU to consult on this case, okay Lou?"

"That would be fine Lenny."

"You could hold a press conference just to notify the public that your department is asking women ages from 18 to 45 to be more observant of their surroundings and don't go out alone. Try not to use the word predator unless the press brings it up."

"Mike and Leon are at the home of our last victim as we talk."

"Ask Mike and Leon if they can learn about this victim's daily routine. Who were they friendly with, what kind of lifestyle, did they live. This will be helpful to the Agents who work in the BAU or anyone I might have to call to consult on this case. Once again, at the FBI we call this victimology."

"Lenny, how long will it be before we hear from the BAU?"

"If you give me your home phone number I can have someone call you this evening."

"I should give you Mike's phone number, I have him heading the investigation."

"Okay Lou, give me his phone number and I'll have someone from the BAU call him."

Captain Costello gives his friend Agent Wolf the cell phone number for Detective Mike Fisher and suggests to Agent Wolf that it would be better if the BAU called Fisher directly but Detective Fisher never hears from the BAU. Captain Costello is concerned that the un-sub is going to kill even more women then they did a few years earlier. The unsub is more confident now than he was then." Detective Fisher and Leon are at the scene of the second homicide in two days. Again, the victim was tied up, raped, and sodomized over and over again, then murdered. She too is a brunette and very attractive. This victim too was laid out as to show remorse.

Surprisingly, this victim turned out to be older then previous victims. This victim, Diane Shelby has brown hair with some light brown highlights. She is fairly thin and has taken pretty good care of herself with the exception that she smoked cigarettes. The assistant coroner believes that she never put up a fight or was unable to. That maybe she was drugged first? At the time of her death she was wearing makeup and lipstick. The detectives looked around the home of the victim for clues and photos they hoped might lead them to bring their un-sub to justice. They found plenty of photos of the victim with family members and possibly friends. Maybe one of them snapped because she had no interests in them?

Meanwhile, Amy receives a call from her sister and they have made plans to get together for lunch on Saturday and so her sister can take Amy to the once converted warehouse where her sister was working on a secret project. Detective Fisher tries to call Amy but she doesn't answer. He wonders if she is safe. Did she go to meet with her sister? Amy signed out of work at 3:30 PM and didn't say where she was going. Fifteen minutes goes by and Mike's cell phone rings and its Amy. "Are you alright Amy?"

"Absolutely Mike. I left work, went to the supermarket, came home and decided to do some cooking. I was trying to call you fifteen minutes ago but I got a busy signal."

"I was trying to call you and then you called me and that's why you got a busy signal."

"Is everything okay?"

"Everything is just fine. I'm at another crime scene. Another woman was found tied up. She was raped, sodomized, and murdered like the other female victims."

"So our un-sub is a serial killer."

"Absolutely. This woman looks similar to our last victim."

"Do you have photos I can look at?"

"Yes. I'll ask Leon to copy photos onto a flash drive for you."

"Did you ask Captain Costello if he is going to have the FBI get involved?"

"Yes I did, and Captain Costello told me he was going to call Agent Wolf and ask him if the BAU will assist us and he probably has done so."

"Great! This isn't my field of expertise, my degree in psychology was to work with children from broken families and with children and teenagers who were abused both psychologically and sexually."

"Don't worry Amy you'll do well in this new position. I have confidence in you."

"Maybe when I see some of the photos Mike, I will be able to assist you with this investigation. I do believe that the un-sub you are looking for remains calm and organized. He just loves to have power over women. The un-sub you are looking for was turned down by ladies that he was attracted to and most likely has suffered some form of psychological break. He might be crying out for help, but he's probably a narcissist because he now thinks that he is superior to these women and law enforcement officers."

"Are you kidding me Amy?" Didn't you tell me that you are the one who thought that you were not the right person for this position but listen to yourself." Amy tells Mike, "I might be wrong."

That evening Amy is busy cooking up some soup while eating a salad when the phone rings. This is Mike and I would like to join you for dinner Amy."

"Why aren't you here yet?" Mike tells Amy, "Amy, I have some photos from the two most recent homicides plus photos from a few years ago."

"Okay Mike, I'll take a look at the photos." Amy is looking for more then that. She wants for the two of them to spend the rest of their lives together. Mike is also interested in spending the rest of his life with Amy, this woman he can't stop thinking about. "Amy, I really need your help to come up with new clues or ideas that will help bring the un-sub to justice."

"So Mike, You and Leon feel that you are getting closer to closing this case."

"There are too many similarities to the victims that should lead the police and FBI right to the home of where the un-sub lives or works."

The problem is, that both the Egg Harbor Police and the FBI failed just a few years earlier in developing a better profile of this un-sub because the un-sub never left enough evidence where they left the remains of their victims, and there was no DNA evidence. The FBI agents at the time determined that the un-sub made their victim take a shower or the un-sub bathed their victims while they were drugged or shortly after the un-sub killed their victims.

CHAPTER 14

AMY IS FORCED TO FACE

While Amy is waiting for Mike to come to her home, the phone rings and it's her sister Ellen. "Hi Amy, are we still on for Saturday?"

"As far as I know we are."

"Good, I have something I want to share with you and you can follow me in your car."

"What's the big secret Ellen?"

"I can't just tell you, I have to show you Amy. You won't believe what I've been able to do. It's going to change the way people look at me, and what I've been working on is going to blow your mind. You are going to look at things differently. You are going to be like a different person when you see what I've been able to do."

"You're not going to give me a hint?"

"No Amy, you have to see it all for yourself."

"What time do you want to get together on Saturday Ellen?"

"Remember, I like for us to meet at Giovanni's Best of Italy on Tilton Road. How about 12:30 PM." Amy, "That sounds fine Ellen. See you then."

The doorbell rings and Mike is at the door. Amy welcomes him in with open arms. Amy has finished cooking the soup and breaks out some crackers while Mike didn't just bring photos from the two recent crime scenes and a couple photos from crime scenes dating back to three years ago; he also brought a bottle of red wine for them to share after dinner.

After finishing dinner Mike and Amy Go over the photos from the most recent homicides and Amy notices similarities in the photos. "All the female victims had similar hairstyles, they were brunettes and their hair was the same length. This un-sub is delusional and this means their likely a narcissist because this un-sub wants to have power over their victims and these victims remind this un-sub of at least one other woman who refused his advances. This un-sub wants us to believe they have remorse but they don't and can't because they're a psychopath."

"So were looking for someone who has no regards for human life. Does this mean that our un- sub is also a sociopath and not just a psychopath, since they have no empathy?"

"That's probably correct. As I said before Mike, I never received any training in profiling. "That's okay Amy. Give yourself some credit. We'll have to write down the amount of time we worked on this. You should get paid."

"Just tell the captain Mike, I just want the credit for it"

"You want for us to make love again tonight?"

"Why don't you sit here for awhile and relax Mike while I put something more comfortable on."

"Okay Amy." In 10 minutes Amy walks into the living room wearing the robe she had on the last time she and Mike made love together.

"I loved how you took it slowly the last couple of times Mike. I love you."

"Why don't you sit down here next to me Amy?" The two lovers sit on the sofa kissing when Mike moves his hands from her cheeks down to her shoulders. Mike and Amy continue kissing, Mike holds Amy's arms and slowly brings her head down on the pillow lying against the armrest and he is on top of her still kissing her. Amy makes it easy for Mike to take control and caress her, to love her. Amy can't believe that making love with Mike is better every time.

It's Friday and it's New Years Eve. Mike and Amy decide to have Mike's parents, brother and sister in-law over for dinner and invite Amy's sister over as well. Amy's father lives in New York with his second wife and her mother is spending New Years with a male friend. Everyone has a good time and after the ball drops bringing in the New Year everyone leaves. Mike and Amy spend another night together. On New Years Day, Mike will be getting together with Leon for a game of racket ball while Amy will be having lunch with her sister and will learn what Ellen has been working on.

Saturday Morning and it's the beginning of a new year. Mike left Amy's place after eating a light breakfast. Amy has cleaned up a little around her home and getting ready to meet her sister for lunch. She gets into her Cadillac SRS and drives to the Italian restaurant she and her sister agreed to during the week. She and Ellen order a small pizza and soft drinks. While Amy uses the ladies room at the restaurant her sister waits for her to comeback to the table. Amy wants to know what Ellen has been up to but Ellen tells her it's a surprise. Amy is intrigued by what Ellen has been working on. "Ellen, you told me that you have been working on a project but haven't even hinted to me what you have been working on. I'm your sister Ellen and you can't even give me a hint."

"That would ruin my surprise Amy. If I told you even the slightest thing about the project I've been working on, I might give something away. I want it to be a surprise."

"Have you spoken to mom lately?"

"Yes Amy, I talk to mom all the time. You should call her Amy."

""We talk on the phone a couple of times a week and had lunch together a few weeks ago."

"I didn't know that?"

"Now that were done eating Ellen, are you finally going to share with me what you have been working on?"

"Of course Amy. Lets pay the check and get out of here. You can follow me."

The two ladies pay for their lunch, leave the restaurant, and Ellen gives Amy the address where they are going in case the traffic doesn't allow for Amy to follow Ellen to the building where she has been working on her project. They get into their automobiles and drive over to the converted warehouse. After arriving at the building, Ellen enters a code to disarm the alarm system. The two ladies walk into the building when Ellen opens a door and invites Amy to enter. After entering the main entrance, Amy is looking around and what does she see? As she walks further down the aisle she sees what looks like large tubes and stainless steel tables with lights over them. She sees what looks like bathtubs but there are tables hanging over two of the tubs. Finally Amy comes to a large tube and sees what looks like a woman in the tube or glass chamber in a standing position. She is standing in a liquid filled tube and Amy is now horrified. Amy could have never imagined why her sister would build such a project and conduct experiments on people or are they people? "Why do you look so horrified Amy?"

"Was that woman a human being and what is this about?" Ellen tells Amy, "I am working on an idea that will allow for more woman to give birth to healthier and intelligent babies. Not only that Amy, I have been able to help both men and women who have been dealing with serious disabilities that have resulted in being restricted to wheel chairs for most of their lives or who had to use canes to walk with and now are free to live their lives without the use of a cane or even a walker. I learned how to use DNA and their own antibodies within their own bodies to free them from any pain many have suffered. "I feel dizzy Ellen, what did you put in the drink I had?"

"You just had a little medicine that will allow you to relax and I'm going to help you to this bed over here. Hold onto me and relax Amy. Now I'll help you onto the bed. Are you feeling more relaxed?"

"Yes I am Ellen."

"Good. I want you to relax. No, I'm not going to put you in one of those tubes."

"What do you want from me Ellen, and why would you do this to me, I'm your sister?"

"You need to relax Amy."

"What are you going to do with me Ellen?"

"I want to take fluids from you so that I can re-produce your genes."

"Stop this Ellen, this isn't right."

"Just stay still Amy."

"You're hurting me Ellen. Oh! Oh! Please stop."

"Amy, you are making this more difficult for me. I'm going to have to give you a shot to quiet you down. After this I'm going to lower you in that bathtub."

"Please stop Ellen, We're sisters aren't we."

"Yes we are but you are the perfect candidate for this experiment."

"What are you going to try and do?"

"I'm going to try and reproduce you. I don't even need to take anything else from you."

"This experience is like some of those horror flicks. Please stop this Ellen, you're hurting me."

"You're giving me a difficult time Amy."

After Ellen is done extracting fluids she needed from her sister, she slides Amy onto a table and moves Amy to one of the bathtubs that she is about to prepare and place Amy into the tub. Ellen turns on the water and pours in a chemical that will cause Amy to become numb. She won't be able to move, she won't be able to fight back because she won't even be able to feel her arms or legs much less be able to move them. Ellen tells her sister that any seamen from Mike will progress more quickly through her body now.

She will most likely become pregnant in a matter of a week or so. The baby should be perfectly normal and intelligent. "How do you know that Mike won't show up?"

"I shut your phone off when you weren't looking in the restaurant and also, your phone won't send any signals from inside this building so Mike isn't going to know where you are. Wait until you tell him you are pregnant. None of the drugs on the market will stop you from becoming pregnant. You know how most guys feel about women who get pregnant and they haven't made any plans for a baby. I'm not doing this to hurt you Amy. You are very intelligent, beautiful and cute. You're my sister. I want to see if I can use your genes to create another person just like you. I'm not angry with you Amy, I'm proud of you and what you have accomplished.

CHAPTER 15

WHERE IS AMY

Long after Mike has finished playing racket ball, he finds that Amy isn't home and she isn't answering her phone. He calls Leon since Leon is a computer whiz and asked him if he can find out where Amy is at by tracking her phone. Leon learns that Amy's cell phone has been off for hours. Leon does learn two important things. First, Amy was at an Italian restaurant in Northfield, and though her phone was shut off around the time she was at the restaurant Leon believes he can find where Amy is. Second, Leon then learns with the new technology the department has use of, Leon is able to learn that Amy is at a building that was once a warehouse and converted into a Laboratory. The Global Positioning Satellite in her SRS allows for Leon to track where Amy's SUV has been and where it is presently located.

"Mike, I have a feeling that we better get over to the building and find out what's going on."

"I wonder why Amy would go there. I'm worried, Leon. Let's meet at the WAWA and go in one car. Don't you think we should take some backup with us?"

"I think we should go there first and then see if we need to call for backup."

"Okay Leon. Maybe we should call the Captain?"

"Now, that I agree with. I think the captain would get pissed at us if something strange were going on and he wasn't called."

"I'll call the captain and ask if he wants to meet us at the WAWA." Mike entered the cell phone number to call the captain and he gets the voice mail message that his boss is unable to answer and leave a message. Then Mike decides to text his boss and asks if he wants to meet he and Leon at the WAWA where they go to for coffee, that Amy is missing and could be at a building that was converted into a laboratory. Mike decides to text his captain to please reply if possible. A few minutes later Captain Costello calls Mike and tells him that he will meet he and Leon at the WAWA in 5 minutes. Mike calls Leon to inform him that the captain will meet them. Shortly after arriving at the WAWA, Leon and Mike meet up with the captain and inform their boss what Leon has learned using the new technology Egg Harbor Township purchased at a discount rate since the department is participating in a new program. They tell their boss that Amy might be in trouble and in a building that was converted from a warehouse to a laboratory.

Now the two detectives along with their captain are on their way to the laboratory that is located in an office complex. The warehouse was once used for office supplies. Ten minutes later the detectives and their captain arrive. The doors are locked but they notice through some windows there are lights on in the building. Detective Fisher goes over to the car opens the trunk and takes out a small kit. He takes one of the tools out and uses it to unlock one of the doors to the building. The two detectives and Captain Costello are now in the laboratory and walking slowly while trying to stay quiet so no one hears them. Meanwhile Ellen had already told her sister that she would feel like brand new after the chemical wore off and she was out of the tub then she disappears. A short time later Mike sees Amy lying flat on a stainless steel table with her eyes closed as though she is dead but notices she is breathing. His eyes filled with tears.

While Mike stays with Amy and calls for a paramedic unit, Captain Costello and Leon walk around the laboratory to see if anyone is still on the premises. Leon finds what looks like a dark collared hair and places it in a plastic tube to give to the lab. Amy is unconscious and Mike has flash backs of the times they spent together. A short time later, Captain Costello and Leon walk up and stand next to Mike. Captain Costello puts his left hand on Mike's right shoulder to let him know he is there in support of Mike and Amy. Leon tells Mike that Amy's breathing and eye movements should be a good sign that Amy should be okay. Leon asks Mike "Would it be okay with you Mike if I check Amy out?" Leon use to work with an EMS (Emergency Medical Service) while going to school. Mike asks Leon "Please see if you can do something for Amy or be honest with me if it's too late. "Were going to get the person who did this Mike. This person is one hell of a dark genius. If this person would do this to a law enforcement officer what would they do to another citizen?" Leon, "I hear sirens, the paramedics must be pulling in to the lot."

"Detectives, we'll talk more later."

"Okay Captain." Leon says. The paramedics are lead over to Amy by Detective Jackson and begin to check Amy out.

TO BE CONTINUED.

www.ingramcontent.com/pod-product-compliance
Lightning Source LLC
Chambersburg PA
CBHW051231210726
48290CB00003B/901